Parting Gifts

By

Tracy Tripp

For my husband, Steve.
Thanks for your patience and for making me
believe in possibilities.

PROLOGUE
The Day Of
Sarah

If I would have kept a diary, if I would have been able to lift a pencil when it was over, if I could have seen into the minds of all the people I loved, this is what I would have said:

Today, I chose to change everything. Today, I destroyed a friendship. A friendship based on love and respect morphed, with a simple screech of a tire, into a bond of secrets, lies, and responsibility. Today, had I been able to look into my husband's eyes, I would have seen the darkness that had never been there before, the darkness when he looked at me, the darkness that would cut me to my core for the rest of my days. Today, I began a slow but undeniable path toward estranging my only daughter, pushing her to the side like an unwanted burden. Beyond all that, beyond all that seems conceivable or recognizable in my otherwise ordinary life, I killed my son.

CHAPTER 1
Present Day
Sarah

Four decisions. As Sarah lay sunken and defeated in a bed that no longer offered comfort, she could only think about how four decisions would shape her life. Three of the decisions, life had already sealed in eternity. Fate was like a tree branching out. For each step she took in one direction, her next move seemed to be determined by increasingly despairing options leading her to this moment.

Sarah was only sixty-four-years-old, yet her body was that of an eighty-year-old woman. Gray hair had prematurely overtaken her once shiny black crown. Her skin was ashen from years of smoking, and if it weren't for the oxygen tank, she would still be lighting up. Sarah glanced over at it as though it held her captive, and only death could relieve her of it. Her last visit to her doctor confirmed that there were only months left, six at best.

She had one decision left to make. One last throw of the dice, hoping to find a single branch of her tree that still had life left in it. Thinking back at the choices she had already made immobilized her.

It had been decades since she trusted her decisions. Her last one, the very worst one, stopped the pulse of her existence. Now she had to decide if she could find the happiness that she once knew so that death was not so terrifying.

Sarah heard a familiar knock at her screen door. A feeling of helplessness overcame her, a response that had been well earned. The soothing voice of her lifetime friend rang through the house sweeter than church bells.

"Morning, Sunshine!" Mary exclaimed. Sarah was sure Mary still believed a smile could chase away all darkness.

"Morning," Sarah grumbled back.

Mary stood before her wearing her tan khakis and starched white blouse. As usual, golden accessories adorned her. She had her hair dyed only yesterday and diligently applied makeup to complete her look. It didn't surprise Sarah that people often mistook Mary for a woman ten years younger. Sarah wondered what Mary must think of her sparse, graying hair and flowery, thin nightgown. COPD had aged her, but even more than that, she knew that she had stopped enjoying living many years before. Much like an empty house, Sarah had begun to break down. She didn't even care about her life ending but feared that nothing awaited her on the other side.

Sarah would stay in her flowery nightgown for the day since getting dressed made her breathless and grooming her hair, much less coloring it, seemed pointless. She watched Mary as she searched through her closet for clothes that they both knew Sarah would dismiss.

"Why do you bother finding me clothes, Mary? I already burned through my visitor's list for the day."

"Well, it's a good thing, too, since you haven't bought anything new in years."

"That's because I've spent all my money on exercise equipment."

"Um."

Sarcasm had become a welcome friend to both women. It allowed their conversation to skim the surface of the waters without ever making a ripple.

At one time, these two girls skipped gingerly through the fields behind Sarah's house, searching for wild strawberries. Both were full of such happiness and hope. How was it that time had treated them so differently? Sarah had borne witness to Mary changing from a girl in pigtails to a girl in Cover Girl makeup, from a young wife to a middle-aged mom, from a student to a nurse. She remained a pillar of strength for everyone around her as she smiled when she wanted to cry and shed off rumors that would have destroyed most others.

Mary retired from nursing and immediately became Sarah's caregiver. They had been friends through many things, but now their friendship was necessary for Sarah's very existence. Mary was there to help Sarah to her chair in the morning and back to her bed at night. She was there to check on her during the day and to help get her meals. As Sarah's disease became progressively tedious and challenging for both women, Sarah wondered when the strands of friendship would break. Never-the-less, Mary continued to stay by her side as she always had with anyone that she felt she could save. Sarah liked to believe that through her, Mary would be given her free pass to heaven so that her existence would hold some value.

The floor of the bedroom was no longer even, and it creaked and moaned as Mary moved around the room, opening shades and brushing the dust off the furniture with her hand. The once tan carpeting was dingy beige, and she wondered if somewhere under the old furniture, she could find a glimpse of what it once was. She glanced around at the mismatched bedroom set she had once dreamed of replacing.

Slowly, Sarah sat up on the bed, brushing her weary feet across the coarse carpet, breathing in and out of the nasal cannula that allowed a small amount of comfort. Mary was prepared for her to move slowly. She patiently waited as Sarah adjusted herself on the double bed. Only one side of the bed was disheveled. The other lay quiet and untouched.

Mary circled the room, letting her hand run gently across the picture frames where the faces of their shared past stared back at them. It was both comforting and painful to look back at so many memories, smiling faces that stood frozen in time, not yet knowing how their futures would take such dark turns. Sarah watched as Mary stopped in front of a picture of Sarah's late husband, Andy, a man they both loved. Her hand gently brushed across his face, not knowing or maybe not caring that Sarah was watching.

Mary moved toward the dresser to where a picture of a young man of sixteen sat upon a doily. His joyful eyes held so much promise that Sarah had to look away to avoid the pain. Mary's hands found the picture of a young woman who, in many ways, resembled a younger Sarah but only in looks. The face was one that Sarah once cherished, but now her image only brought pain and regret.

So many images of long-gone smiling faces pierced through her soul. They were only ghosts now that haunted Sarah as she had aged to a needy old woman. As Sarah watched Mary absorb the past, she saw a soft smile enlighten her face. There wasn't any pain in her eyes, and Sarah envied her for that. Not able to stand the memories any longer, she called out to Mary.

"I'm ready now."

Mary turned toward Sarah, her mind straddling the past and present.

"All right, honey, let's get you up then. Remind me to thank you when my thighs start to look like I'm thirty again."

"Your thighs didn't look that great when you were thirty."

"Speak for yourself, old lady," Mary said. "I didn't secretly call you thunder thighs for nothing."

"You really weren't that secretive about it."

"You're probably right about that." They laughed enough to acknowledge the humor behind their jabs.

"All right, on the count of three. One, two, three, and up."

Mary's body, the same age as Sarah's, found the strength to lift the parts of her old friend that Sarah could not raise alone. With the help of a walker, they shuffled across the floor and out into the short hallway leading to the living room. Sarah was carefully eased into her worn recliner as if she were a rag doll about to tear. The familiar smells of her living room rushed toward her; garlic and onions, dust, and stuffiness. It was a smell that was home but not necessarily pleasant. It only reminded Sarah of the fading memories being replaced by the aroma of age.

7

Sarah looked around at her living room. She saw a small ding on the wall that was half-hidden by the couch. It was a reminder of the only time she saw her husband become physically angry. The outdated curtains could not negate the wallpaper that was peeling in the corners. The recliner had molded to fit her body now tender from sitting in the same position every day. She craved relief, but what healing was there? Her time had become so limited that looking forward only caused swells of anxiety.

Mary went into the tiny kitchen to prepare some toast and black decaf coffee. It was all Sarah's stomach could tolerate in the morning. The white countertop that was no longer regularly scrubbed showed the stains of life. The burn mark left from one of Sarah's favorite days of her life so many years before, still holding its place like a beacon in a storm. So many times, Sarah had run her hand across the mark, hoping the action could transport her back to that moment.

Mary opened the refrigerator door and searched for butter through the containers of Meals on Wheels meals. Anger rose in Mary as another sign of her friend's tortured soul emerged before her. Some days Mary wanted to run as far away as she could. The darkness of Sarah's existence smothered her, but she knew that this was what she needed to do. Mary had to see Sarah to the end if either of them stood any chance of finding peace. After all, didn't she owe Sarah that? She dug deep for the last drop of cheer in her voice before speaking.

"Honestly, Sarah, this refrigerator makes me not want to eat either. I really need to come over and clean this thing out for you."

Without responding, Sarah cleared off a spot on her cluttered tray for her breakfast. Her hand grazed a letter from Amanda before it fluttered to the floor. She let it go. It only hurt a little now, letting Amanda fall away from her. She brushed off the pain like an annoying bug. Mary set Sarah's breakfast down in front of her and noticed the letter. She picked it up with an irritated sigh and tucked it in her pocket. Sarah was thankful for the lack of comment and was only slightly curious about what she did with the letters she often confiscated.

"I'm running some errands and then grabbing lunch. Can I bring something back for you?"

Sarah thought desperately, but what could she want? She often felt like her life was like a trip to the grocery store. She spent her time looking around for what she came for and couldn't find anything. Searching the shelves, all that had once appealed to her looked back at her with bland and unappealing eyes. She looked at the food with no craving to taste it, at the wine with no desire to drink it, at the people with no desire to know them. She couldn't go through the imaginary doors without going through checkout, but there was nothing in her cart. Nothing in her life was worth carrying with her. She felt trapped, not knowing why she had come in the first place.

"I don't need anything, but thank you. I would love your company for lunch, though."

"Then, I'll be here. Except, I'm craving something special today, so you're either going to have to watch me eat it or join me."

"I'll work on an appetite, then."

Once Mary had gone, Sarah felt the weight of having to fake happiness lifted. She was unaware of how bad she was at faking it and how she made her dear friend work so hard at being happy around her. She reached for the remote, and the day began to move not by the clock but by the television programs.

It had done that for many years, long before Bob Barker aged to a gray-haired man and disappeared from her living room, bringing a new generation of hosts and contestants. It was hard saying goodbye, for he linked her to her past, a past of quiet lunches with Andy, of toddlers and teens. It seemed Bob was a witness to it all, and she felt the loss like that of an old friend. She stared at the square box that tried to keep her connected and drifted into thoughts of the past.

CHAPTER 2

Decision One

1956

Sarah

Bill Cullen introduced the guest of *The Price is Right* while Mary and Sarah, two young girls the age of seven, sat in front of the television. It was Sarah's turn to wear her father's black-rimmed reading glasses so that they could resemble the host.

"Introducing the next contestant, Mary Allen." Sarah taped up the pictures of the magazine ads that they would be bidding on, while she glanced over the glasses that made everything a blur.

"Today, Mary gets to bid on a new bed and dresser."

"Oh, Bill, they are just lovely." Before she could put in her bid, the quiet clipping sound of the mower silenced giving way to the sturdy footfalls of her father's boots as he approached. The girls scrambled to put his glasses back on the end table where they belonged. Then they quickly turned to hide their hands behind their backs to block the evidence from Sarah's father, Jason Foster, known mostly as Jay.

The screen door opened and slammed shut with a familiar springy thud. As Jay passed them, he looked at the two conspiring children with one raised eyebrow before entering the kitchen for a glass of water. The two girls stole nervous glances at each other as Sarah's father determined their fate. He walked back by them with the same look, and as the door was about to close behind him, he questioned them.

"Girls, you wouldn't be playing with my glasses again, would you?"

"No, Daddy. No, sir," they innocently chimed together.

Their nervousness was strictly for their entertainment since Sarah was never severely scolded, but then she didn't give much reason for it. She had great respect for her father and was not a child to instigate disapproval. They both let out a deep breath, and the house fell silent for a moment except for the voice of Bill joking with the contestants.

Sarah and her father lived in a modest home together and alone. When Sarah was two-years-old, her mother died in childbirth, taking with her the sister Sarah would never know. In Sarah's mind, she would have been Elizabeth. After five years, Sarah had no memories left of her mother; however, a warmth filled her whenever Sarah thought of her. She kept a picture beside her bed and would kiss it every night before being tucked in by her father, a man that found the courage and love to be both a mother and father. Sarah pictured her mother often and created memories of her own. They were memories, more stolen than created, as she watched her neighbor and her children interact the way she assumed all mothers and daughters would.

After school, or on summer days when her father was at work, she would go to Mrs. Bates' house to play with her girls, Cassie and Pauline. Cassie was four, and Pauline was five. Since Sarah was several years older, playing with them was only out of necessity, and she preferred to think of herself as a mother's helper. Sarah watched as their mother hugged them when they got hurt, made muffins with them for after-school snacks, and acted amazed at each drawing they presented.

These images evolved into memories of the mother she dreamed she would have had. She swam in the warmth of their home, danced in the aromas of motherly perfume, and learned how dearly she missed the woman she never got to know. The home her father created was full of love, but the smell of homemade muffins was traded in for the less pleasant odors of burnt spam and canned corn.

After losing their prop, Mary and Sarah left the land of *The Price is Right* and decided to go into the kitchen to mix lemonade. Mary immediately began measuring out the lemonade as Sarah ran her hand under the kitchen faucet waiting for the old pipes to run cold. One added the sugar as the other added the water in perfect combination forming the sweet taste of summer in their pitcher. They carefully carried it outside to try to sell enough to run to the corner store for a handful of nickel candies.

After an hour of chasing the bees away from the sweet nectar, they had only had two customers, Cassie and Pauline, who had eagerly skipped over with no money to offer. After exchanging annoyed looks, they decided to give them some regardless. As they watched them bounce away, Sarah and Mary knew it was time to close shop and forget about their candy.

Sarah's father headed toward the backyard, and Mary and Sarah took to the trail, running the paths that were created by the mower as if they were part of a labyrinth. They shed their shoes and the freshly cut grass stuck to their feet, turning them into amusing green extensions. They didn't need to speak; instead, they giggled as they ran the paths, throwing their faces up to the bright sunshine. It was as if they already knew they should be soaking it all in while they were young. They ran till they were dizzy with laughter and fell in a heap onto each other.

"Sarah don't go in the house covered with grass clippings," her dad called.

"Okay, Daddy."

They looked down at their transformed feet, and almost in unison knew that their next stop would be the small brook that ran behind her house.

"Daddy, we're running to the brook."

Whether or not he heard her was questionable, but he gave an okay wave. They raced down the path and reached their favorite part of the brook. The water was widest there, and after heavy rains, they would even throw inner tubes in and travel a short way in the current. For the most part, they would merely explore together.

They stood barefoot in the chilly waters, searching through the ripples for crawfish. Each day they would tell themselves they would be brave enough to grab one of the creatures from their quiet resting spot at the bottom of the brook. Each time they found themselves screaming and giggling without ever learning the feel of the crawfish's shell.

"It's your turn, Sarah."

"My turn! But you didn't catch one."

"I tried. He was too fast."

"No, he wasn't. You were scared."

"Then, you do it."

Sarah stared down into the waters. Over and over, she told herself this was going to be the day she caught the crawfish. Finally, she focused in on one, a rather big one as crawfish go. Sarah breathed in and out, trying to slow her racing heart. Suddenly,

15

she lunged toward the creature and felt her foot slip on the moss-covered rocks. She found herself sitting chest-high in the very water that contained the crawfish. Her only thought was of the creature finding his way up her shorts. Sarah began screaming and thrashing as if she were under attack.

When she finally found herself safely on the bank, she noticed Mary doubled over with tearful laughter. The fear gave way to Sarah's outburst of laughter, and the girls were lost yet again in the magic of childhood.

So lost were they in their fun that they did not notice the storm quickly appearing above the treetops. It was only the loud crack of thunder rushing through the sky that alerted them to their impending danger. They stumbled over the slippery rocks to cross back over the brook. On the final step, Sarah slipped again and felt a jagged rock scrape against her skin. She whimpered and grabbed for her injured knee.

Mary was by her side immediately, giving comfort and support. The stinging sensation was quite tolerable, but it had become a habit of Sarah's to accept Mary's compassion. Sometimes it was for Sarah's sake and sometimes Mary's. Sarah knew it was in these moments that Mary was in her element. She needed to be a caretaker like the sun needed to shine.

Her father must have been watching for them because he was standing on the front steps as they approached. He strolled toward them, Sarah's arm around Mary's neck for support. Mr. Foster had also become accustomed to the roles the two girls played and showed it in his lackadaisical approach. The fact that Sarah was still his little girl allowed him some pleasure in playing along with the unimpressive injury.

"Oh my, what has happened to my little princess?"

"She slipped on the rocks when we heard the thunder. I helped her all the way home."

"That doesn't surprise me at all, Mary. Let's get you out of the rain."

"I'll get some ice."

Mary ran into the kitchen. They could hear Mary rifling through the freezer as her father set Sarah on the couch. Looking down at her knee and seeing only a small trickle of blood made her realize the pampering would not last long.

"Oh my, it looks like we're going to have to stitch this up. Mary, run and grab me a needle and thread."

Mary stopped in the doorway with fear in her eyes. She wouldn't have been nearly so afraid if she knew there hadn't been a needle or thread in their house in years.

"You're not going to stitch it," Sarah giggled.

"Well, then what if I do this?"

Her dad grabbed her arms and lifted them, exposing the vulnerable armpit. He didn't have to even touch her. Merely watching his hand hover dangerously above her was enough to set off fits of laughter, so much so that her breath could barely escape.

"I'm better. I promise. Please let me go."

"Okay, then, I think my work here is done."

He gave her one more squeeze and a kiss on the forehead before the girls scrambled off to Sarah's bedroom. Sarah would never know how much Mary envied her for being her father's little girl.

After a dinner of scrambled eggs and toast, the girls slipped into the nightgowns for another summer sleepover. Mary grabbed a handful of *Dick and Jane* books and jumped into the bed.

"Let's take turns reading like last time," Mary suggested.

"I can read *Dick and Jane* on my own, Mary."

"Well, I know you can, but isn't it fun to play teacher?"

"But, you're always the teacher."

"I promise next time you can be."

Sarah's face scrunched up as if to say she didn't believe any of it and then relaxed with an exasperated sigh. Everything seemed to come easy to Mary. Even though Mary wasn't one to brag, Sarah felt envious.

Mary started to read. "'Pretty, Pretty Puff.' That's the title," Mary knowingly informed her friend. "Jane said, 'Where is Sally? I want to find Sally. Where is she? Please help me, Dick. Please help me find Sally.' Your turn, Sarah. Sarah, aren't you going to read?"

Sarah forced herself to look back at the book. "Dick said, 'We will find Sally. She is in the house. Come, Jane. I will help you find Sally.'"

"Good job, Sarah."

"This story is easy," Sarah grumbled but refrained from slamming the book shut and throwing it off the bed. Mary merely rolled her eyes as if she were dealing with a child's tantrum.

"Let's put the book away and tell stories instead," Sarah suggested.

Mary sighed and put the book on her nightstand.

"Okay, you first."

They nestled into the cool, crisp pillowcases and lay face to face. With the superiority factor out of the way, both girls relaxed.

"Let me think a minute," Sarah said.

"Lights out girls. I'll be waking you up early for church."

Sarah's weary eyes welcomed her father's voice.

"We better get to sleep. Are you sure you don't mind coming to church with us?"

"I would never be able to stay over on Saturdays if I didn't go."

"I guess we could always drop you off on the way."

"It's all right."

Sarah smiled at her friend, wondering if maybe she secretly enjoyed going. Then she rolled toward the nightstand where the picture of her mother sat. As always, she picked it up and stared at her for a moment, wondering what it would be like to have her sitting by her bedside, softly brushing her bangs from her face and whispering goodnight. Sarah kissed the stranger she called mother and turned back toward her friend.

"Goodnight, Mary."

"Goodnight, Sarah."

The warm summer night wrapped around the little girls as they drifted off to sleep. Mary was the sweetness in the bland water, her umbrella when it rained, her chosen sister, and even, on occasion, her mother even when she didn't ask for her to be. She knew as they lay there, in their white linen nightgowns and long brown pigtails, that some friendships were meant to last forever.

CHAPTER 3
Present Day
Sarah

How long had it been? Maybe a few hours. Sarah heard Mary's car pulling back into the driveway. Mary came in, waving a bag that smelled of fried chicken. Sarah had become a fan of fried chicken as a child visiting Mary's house. Mrs. Allen made the best fried chicken in town. Not that Sarah would know since she had only eaten hers, but every time she made it, Mary's dad would kiss her on the cheek and say, "Mmm, you make the best fried chicken in town," so maybe it was true.

The smell brought her back as fragrances sometimes can, making it possible to reach into a forgotten part of the brain and reawaken memories long gone. There were so many good memories, but they were buried too deep, and to get to them, she would have to dig through hell.

"I brought an old favorite."

"Oh, yes, I remember it well. Only I didn't use to have to worry about my dentures falling out when I ate it."

"We have gotten old, haven't we?"

"Well, I have. Your body doesn't seem to know you're aging somehow."

"Are you kidding me? I'm winded from carrying the bag in." Sarah knew this not to be true. "At least we don't need to count calories anymore. No one checks you out when you're in your sixties," Mary added.

"I thought the mailman looked at me funny the other day, but then it might have been that I forgot to button up my nightgown."

Mary still threw back her head when she laughed, and she never let an opportunity pass her by. It was a laugh that used to be so contagious.

"Oh dear, I am sorry, but that's not a sight any of us need to be seeing anymore."

They had eaten fried chicken many times at her house until they were old enough to discover boys. Somewhere soon after that, they learned that their waists were supposed to be twenty-two inches in accordance with their thirty-two-inch breasts and hips. They had a long way to go in the breast department, but they figured cutting down on the fried foods might help the waist problem.

Mary was the first to start having more notable crushes on boys, or at least a boy, Dan Hunter. By most any girl's standards, Dan was attractive. To Sarah, he represented commonplace. He was the epitome of the high school girl's dream with good looks, athleticism, popularity, and the precise amount of bad guy to make the girls drool. Maybe it was intimidation, but Sarah never cared for any of it.

To protect their friendship, she faked a crush on his snobbish friend, Matt. The girls waited for the next break in Dan's romance with Kathleen, the girl known for her popularity with the boys. As soon as the break-up rumors began, they would initiate the plan. The first one to get their first kiss got bragging rights for life.

Mary had concocted the four-day masterpiece. Sarah had some serious doubts, but since she was secretly hoping to fail, she kept them to herself. Over the phone, Mary excitedly told her to write down the plan as she quickly rambled off the idea. She scribbled away while rolling her eyes and then promptly tried to end the conversation claiming that dishes were waiting for her.

"Okay. Okay. I'll see you tomorrow. And Sarah..."

"Yeah?"

"Wear something cute."

"Goodbye, Mary."

"Bye."

Sarah glanced over the list before tossing it in the garbage embarrassed that she had bothered to write everything down, knowing they only signified Mary's lack of confidence in Sarah when it came to boys.

Mary's big plan was this:

Day 1: Wait outside the class until Dan and Matt entered. Make sure they made eye contact.

Day 2: Wait outside the class until Dan and Matt entered. Make sure they made eye contact.

Day 3: Try to say hi.

Day 4: Hope the boys make the next move because they had no idea what to do after that.

Sarah could not help but think that for someone as smart as Mary, she could act quite dumb when it came to boys. Maybe her plan was meant to get their attention by acting nonchalant. Either way, she was quite sure that she would have nothing to worry about despite Mary's charm. Her clean reputation would repel him.

Day one came, and they waited nervously. Sarah could see the boys come around the corner. They were always together, much like Mary and Sarah were, a fact that would be beneficial when planning a double date. They were quickly approaching, and Sarah felt her face begin to flush. Mary glanced at her with a disapproving look right before managing a smile directed at Dan. He snagged it like a fish and smiled back. Matt kept walking as if they weren't even there. Sarah was relieved, except she knew she would suffer through some gloating and reprimanding.

Day two, Dan seemed to be noticing Mary as he approached the room, and she skipped right over the eye contact and went onto day three's hi. Matt kept walking.

Day three, Dan stopped in front of them and smiled at Mary.

"Isn't your name, Mary?"

"Yes, yours is Dan, right?"

Sarah concealed a slight eye roll by glancing into the classroom, desperately wanting to disappear into it. She noticed Matt looking at her but not in a way that hinted at interest; he was merely checking out what might be in it for him. He didn't seem excited. Sarah busied herself by counting the squares on the floor. By the time she reached twenty, the conversation was over, and they were rushing to their seats. Sarah couldn't help but notice how Dan kept looking over at Mary during class and how Mary wore a smile that made her a stranger.

Something was unsettling, but Sarah tried to push past it. New experiences often made her nervous. She let the teacher's words blur into background noise for her thoughts, and she realized that, for the first time, she felt like an outsider to Mary's world. The next time she noticed Dan smiling at Mary, she nearly shivered. She felt as if she were watching a hunter and its prey, except the hunter didn't carry a gun, just a smile.

The next morning, Sarah was met by Mary, almost skipping down the hall.

"Dan asked me to the movies, and the best part is he wants you and Matt to join us, which is good because my mom wouldn't let me go alone. I thought we could get ready at my house, and they could pick us up."

She rambled on so fast Sarah could barely keep up with the words. Fear and excitement began to rise from the pit of Sarah's stomach, and she suddenly felt nauseated.

"What day are we going?

"Saturday, I don't even know what movie, but I can't wait."

Saturday arrived too quickly. Mary danced around her room, trying on her new sweater and putting the precise amount of poof in her hair. Sarah could only watch as she tied her scarf around her neck, vibrantly showing off the latest fashions. Her own heart pounded fiercely, making her insecurities more pronounced. She busied herself by picking the balls off her sweater.

The sound of the knock traveled up the stairs. Mary grabbed Sarah's shoulders and began jumping up and down with a muffled cry of excitement. Sarah's body imitated Mary's, yet her eyes clearly showed panic.

"Girls, your friends are here," Mary's mother called up.

Mary looked Sarah squarely in the eye and said, "Tonight, we will get our first kiss."

Pulling themselves together, they descended the stairs to the watchful eyes of Mary's parents, Sarah's father, and two boys that were nearly strangers to them.

Before being released into this new world, Jay bombarded Matt and Dan, or so it seemed, with a list of questions.

"What movie will you be seeing?"

"*The Cincinnati Kid.*"

"Who will be driving?"

"Dan."

"Make sure you are home by 10:00."

"We will," they all answered simultaneously.

Sarah hugged her dad tightly, secretly hoping he would change his mind and tell her not to go. She wasn't so much scared of a first kiss, but it was unsettling to her that it would be with a boy she barely knew, and she wasn't quite sure she was capable of liking. Sarah pictured her first kiss to be with someone she had dreamed about, much like Mary had fantasized about Dan. Maybe she felt she was a little robbed of the excitement Mary was feeling and of something that should have been a beautiful memory. Matt's attitude seemed like he was doing a friend a favor. For a moment, she considered biting him instead but reconsidered when she pictured Mary's reaction.

There was some polite conversation before the movie began, but then all was quiet. The only words spoken were by Dan. When Karl Madden started yelling at Ann-Margaret for cheating in Solitaire, both Sarah and Mary heard him mumble something about typical women. They looked at each other and shrugged it off.

After some time passed of quiet watching, Sarah felt the slight brush of a hand as Dan's arm circled Mary's shoulder followed by a pinch on her leg to make sure she was aware of the move. Within minutes, she felt Matt's arm reach around her making her stomach muscles tighten with anxiety. Her pinch for Mary may have been a little too hard. She slightly leaned in to whisper something to Mary and found her mid-kiss. Sarah stared as if witnessing the end of an era and the beginning of a very unfamiliar one.

As she turned back toward the screen, she felt the soft brush of Matt's hand on her cheek. As she glanced toward him, her lips met his. It was final. She had received her first kiss, and to her surprise, she liked it. Sarah was not quite sure how the movie ended because from that point on, if she was not engaged in a kiss, she was thinking about it. The giddiness that Mary had displayed was seeping through her friend, and Sarah felt this new era had its possibilities. Then again, she was not always a good judge.

When they got to school on Monday, there were giggles and stares, but this time they were not the ones giggling. It wasn't until mid-day that Kathleen slipped Sarah a note that had been circling around the school. In big letters were the words, *Mary Allen is easy.* She immediately tore it up and threw it in the trash, hoping Mary would never know.

"Kathleen, why were you passing that note around? You know it's not true."

"I didn't start the letter. Someone gave it to me."

"It doesn't even matter who started it. You shouldn't be passing it around. Mary's anything but easy, and you know it. I was with them all night. All we did was go to the movies and back home. What do you think took place in a theater?" Sarah was sure she saw relief pass over her face. "You can't hate Mary for going to a movie with Dan. You two are broken up."

Kathleen stared back at Sarah as if weighing facts that were not aligning in her mind, and the realization settled in for Sarah. Mary was about to have her heartbroken.

"Dan and I only had a fight. We did not break up!"

"If that's true, why did he ask Mary to the movies?"

"Maybe because Mary threw herself at him, and he was angry with me. Trust me; he doesn't care about Mary."

As if on command, Dan came around the corner with Matt. Matt walked directly into the classroom with no eye contact. Sarah could have cared less. Then Dan walked right up to Kathleen, put his arm around her, and with smiling faces, they entered the room together. Mary came slowly around the corner. Sarah wanted to protect her from the pain, but she could tell by the way Mary hugged her books tightly to her chest and stared at the floor that she already knew. Why was it so hard to see a tower fall?

Sarah couldn't understand how a boy Mary barely knew could have such an effect on her. She wanted to jump in front of the flying debris and shield her. As usual, she didn't know how to protect her friend the way Mary always seemed to protect her. If only they knew then that they should have run from him like the devil himself, maybe everything would have been different.

Sarah could only watch Mary from a distance that day. She didn't have to tell her to give her space, Sarah just knew. Not until school finished for the day did Mary speak.

"Do you want to go back to my house after school?"

"Definitely."

By dinner, Mary was resurfacing, and whatever pain she experienced would never be discussed. Instead, she helped Sarah with her math, with a bit more of a Catholic school teacher attitude than usual, minus the ruler. Together they picked out what scarf would be right with yet another new sweater and awaited the call for dinner. They ate fried chicken.

CHAPTER 4

1966

M a r y

Mary considered herself intelligent. She was not one to swoon over the most popular guy in school just because he was good looking and played football. With Dan, there was something different. Perhaps it was the way he faced his opponents on the field that drew her to him. He was the starting linebacker known for his vicious hits. Even in the nearby towns, people respected his drive. Coaches would strategize with their players how to best prevent a strike from number twenty-one.

Mary didn't care that he was a star. She needed to know what powered him. Why did he appear so eager to take on the world one person at a time? She wanted to chase away the dark. After the movie, she had laid in bed, smiling at the ceiling until she was sure she could see the sun start to rise. She couldn't wait for Monday to come. Images of walking down the hallway holding hands with Dan consumed her for the rest of the weekend.

Then Monday came. It was not very often that Mary felt inferior. The note and her apparent inability to read Dan had shaken her. Mary's mind tried to wrap itself around this unfamiliar feeling, to see if there was room in her small frame for such negativity. After dinner with Sarah, she decided there was not. When Tuesday came, she held her head high and brushed it off. Smiling, she walked down the hallway as if she was happy that he was back with Kathleen, and because it was Mary, people believed it.

What she wasn't expecting was what happened when she slipped out of class to use the restroom. She heard her name whispered from behind her. When she turned, Dan lightly grabbed her arm and pulled her to a quiet corner.

"Mary, I'm truly sorry about all this. Kathleen heard about the movies and was so upset. I worry about her sometimes. She gets so emotional I just don't know…Anyway, I have to move a bit slower with this."

Mary stared at him with scornful eyes. Despite her anger, something flickered in her heart, maybe hope. "So, what are you saying?"

"Just be patient, please. Kathleen's crazy fragile, and I'm not the kind of guy that breaks hearts easily. I'll let things cool a bit and then make the break. Okay?"

"I guess so."

"Can I call you tonight?"

"Sure."

With a sly smile, he watched her as he peddled back a few steps. "I really enjoyed the other night." Then he turned the corner.

Mary stayed hidden while she caught her breath. She knew she couldn't tell Sarah she spoke with Dan. Sarah could so effortlessly deflate her excitement sometimes. Still, Mary needed Sarah as much as Sarah needed her.

The days passed, and Dan called almost every night. Mary was beginning to love having her little secret. Dan would tell her how he had his eye on her long before the movies and that he only felt responsible for Kathleen. He would whisper into the phone how much he enjoyed kissing her and how he couldn't wait to do it again. Mary's body pulsed with excitement. The sound of his voice rattled her, and she could no longer think clearly. In her mind, it was acceptable to be the other woman, and, in fact, wasn't she helping Dan be considerate of Kathleen's feelings? She was still a good person.

Mary and Sarah would go to the football games on the weekend, and Mary secretly watched Dan tear up the field like an angry animal, her animal. She purposely stayed away from the cheerleaders. Kathleen, bouncing around in her cheerleading getup unaware of her position, tugged at Mary's conscience. Mary had gone to school with Kathleen since grade school, and their level of friendship varied from year to year. Kathleen had always been popular if not a bit snooty. Mary would have never guessed that she was so naive and so breakable.

It only took three weeks before Dan called Mary and said it was over with Kathleen. Dan said she cried for quite some time and kept asking why. All Mary cared about was that it was over. She knew Kathleen would get over it soon enough.

Mary had a hard time feeling sorry for her after due to how she acted when he dumped her after the movie. The rumor that went around the school was that Dan had been too forceful, and Kathleen ended it. Dan convinced Mary that they should let her paint whatever picture she wanted if it made it a smoother transition. He was glad to be done with her. The only thing that concerned Mary was that if she wanted to move forward with Dan, Sarah would need to know.

As she suspected, Sarah looked at her with disbelief. Mary tried to explain the situation, and Sarah pretended to listen. She knew by Sarah's lack of response that Sarah would not support her relationship with Dan. For the first time, Mary felt a distance between them, and instead of wanting to run to her friend, she found herself wanting to seek out Dan, not caring if she was jeopardizing a piece of their friendship. Sarah would get used to it. When Mary told Dan about Sarah's reaction, he pulled her into him.

"Mary, you know she is jealous of you. It's hard for her to watch you having a boyfriend when no one is showing interest in her."

"She's not jealous of me," Mary insisted, even though, she wondered. "Why don't we try to set her up with Matt again?"

"I don't think that's gonna work out." Mary studied his face, pleading with her eyes. "Mary, she just isn't like you. She clings to you. I mean, really, Mary, it's pathetic."

"She doesn't cling to me. We've been best friends forever."

"Really? I thought best friends looked out for each other and were happy for each other. Trust me. If you let her, she will try to break us up."

"She's not going to break us up. I wouldn't break up with you just because she wants me to."

"Prove it." With that, he planted a kiss on her head and headed to class.

Every time Mary spoke with Sarah, she thought of Dan's words. Her sullenness had become an annoying assurance that Dan was probably right. When Dan asked her to another movie, she agreed to go without Sarah. His friends and their girlfriends would be there. She tried not to let Sarah know her plans for fear she would have to tell her that Matt wouldn't go with her again. She would sit with Dan, acutely aware that she was an outsider in his group. The girls were apparently friends of Kathleen's, and

Mary knew they would never accept her as one of them. That was fine because she had Dan. Slowly, she felt her outside world drifting away.

She watched Sarah becoming friends with other girls. Occasionally, she would want to go to her, but Dan would hold her hand until the moment passed. For the first few months, Dan showered her with affection and made her feel like the center of his world. She became dependent on him for companionship, and she let herself believe it was the natural order of things. Eventually, Sarah and she had to grow apart enough to allow men in their lives. Maybe she and Dan had a real future?

Mary could almost forget about the darkness in Dan's eyes that drew her to him, but sometimes on the phone at night, she would hear his parents. His father would be yelling something too mumbled to decipher. She was quite sure he was drunk. His mom was quieter, but Mary could make out her timid voice in the background.

Whenever the fighting happened, Dan would end the conversation quickly. She knew he must be embarrassed, and she desperately wanted him to believe that she loved him no matter what secrets his family hid. She knew, for the time, it was best to act like she didn't hear. After one particularly loud fight, Mary felt a change in Dan. When she planted a kiss on his cheek in the hallway, he put his hand on her to distance himself.

"Seriously, Mary? We're seniors, and sometimes you can act so pathetically young." Mary was frozen, stricken. "Sorry, but it's a bit embarrassing when you bound up to me like you're ten. Just be a lady is all I'm sayin."

With that, he gave her backside a small slap and headed to class. She saw Sarah huddled with a group of girls down the hall and was thankful her back was to her. Mary didn't want to have a witness to her disgrace.

For the rest of the week, Dan was a bit standoffish but didn't criticize her again. She felt like he was slipping away, and Mary found herself wanting to cling to him like a lifeboat. She had trusted him when he led her into these lonely waters. No one could have been more surprised when she found herself crying during their phone call.

"Now what, Mary?"

"Nothing, I just feel like you're pulling away from me."

"Or are you suddenly becoming clingy?" Silence fell over the phone. "I'm sorry, Mary. I just…You don't understand what I am going through at all. I don't mean to take it out on you."

"Why don't you tell me? I want to know every part of you, even the bad stuff."

"Be careful of what you wish for."

"I love you, Dan. You can tell me anything."

"Someday, Mary. Someday maybe you'll know everything."

DAN

Dan hung up the phone. Mary wanted to know everything. He laughed out loud. Would she want to know that his father used the belt on him whenever he broke a minor rule? Would Mary genuinely want to hear about how he had to watch his dad push his mom around until she couldn't stand back up? That every time he was on the field, he pictured fighting back. Or best of all, that a son could hate his own mother. He hated what women stood for. Weakness. Too weak to even protect their own children. Whimpering fools. They were good for one thing, and eventually, he would get that from Mary.

MARY

For days after their conversation, Dan seemed distant, and Mary followed like a puppy dog desperate for attention. She knew what it must look like, still she told herself that no one understood them. Dan needed her. She would break through the anger and sadness. She would make them both happy in the end. Slowly, the playful Dan that she craved would part the dark clouds with his smile. Mary was sure of it.

If only Sarah could get to know the Dan that she fell in love with. If only she could have her best friend and boyfriend. For the time, Mary was just thankful that it had been a great week at school. Dan gave her all his attention, held her hand on the way to class, and instead of driving off at the end of school with his friends, he offered Mary a ride.

As Mary stared at the phone, she could not help but think back to sitting in front of her house in Dan's car. Her mind was spinning, and she desperately wanted to talk with Sarah. Dan was supposed to be just dropping her off, except he acted like he was not in any hurry to leave.

"Do you want to come in for a few minutes?" Mary asked. "You can't stay long because my mom gets home shortly. I wouldn't be allowed to leave my room for a month if she knew I let a boy come in the house while she wasn't home."

"Oh my, I like it when you live dangerously," Dan said with a mischievous grin. "I promise I won't stay long. Let's go."

Mary reached for her door handle. She was suddenly regretting her decision. "Maybe we should park around the corner?"

Dan started the car and eased into a spot out of sight. The image of her mother's disappointed face pushed itself into Mary's mind, and she shoved it back out.

"We better go now if we're going."

They raced to the door with nervous glances over their shoulders. Once inside, Mary offered Dan a soda, but he answered with silence.

"Dan, Dan, where are you?"

"So, which room is yours?" The sound of the opening and closing of bedroom doors upstairs followed his voice. Mary's heart stopped.

"Dan, you can't go up there. Seriously, please come down."

"I bet this one's it. I love the pink. It makes you seem so innocent."

Mary raced up the stairs two at a time, found Dan, and started pleading while pulling his sleeve. Dan only laughed, wrapped his arms around her waist, and dragged her onto the bed with him.

"Dan, seriously! I'll be in so much trouble if my mom comes home."

"Listen, we can hear the cars passing. If your mom pulls in, I can be downstairs and out the back door before she reaches the porch."

"I don't know, Dan."

"Relax. Do you think I'm gonna bite you?"

"I'm not sure," Mary said with a slight smile breaking through her fear.

"It must be nice having this beautiful home and parents that give a shit."

Mary waited a moment, hoping he would add more. She craved to know the reason for the darkness. Dan only searched the room for a moment with a distant look.

"What's your home like?"

"Well, I guess it would be okay if anyone paid much attention to it. My mom's always working, and my dad's always... Never mind."

"Dan, you can share anything with me."

"I don't talk to anyone about them." Dan moved a little closer to her so that their bodies pressed together.

"I like to share with you, though. Do you like to share with me?"

Mary's breath stuck in her throat, and she felt her face become flushed. "Tell me more about your dad."

"My dad," Dan started with an edge in his throat, "is nothing but a drunk that slaps my mom around."

Mary thought she saw a tear forming in his eye, and he brushed his face with the back of his hand. When he put his hand back down, he rested it on Mary's hip. She started to feel his fingers finding their way to her flesh at the base of her shirt.

"Dan, we should get back downstairs."

"I told you we would hear your mom coming. Besides, I thought we were sharing." His warm, firm hand that had settled on the small of her back was creeping around her rib cage.

"Dan, I'm not really..."

"I've never felt so close to anyone. It means so much to me to be able to talk to you." His mouth closed over hers forcefully enough that she wouldn't be able to talk, and his hand shot up her shirt. She tried to move, but his one leg went around her enough that before she could do anything, she felt his hand slide under her bra and had her breast cupped in his hand.

The sound of a car motor froze them momentarily. His hand stood firm on her as he spoke.

"I'm glad you shared with me, too. That's what makes us a couple, Mary, and you do want that, don't you?"

The question hung before her. Dan pulled his hand away, and as he promised, fled out the back door without a witness.

Mary found herself staring at the phone. She needed her friend. She needed Sarah to understand and tell her everything would be all right, but she dreaded the disapproving silence. Mary couldn't handle that, especially since her mind kept whispering, *Run!*

CHAPTER 5

1 9 6 7

S a r a h

L ooking back, Sarah knew she should have guessed by the way Mary had been rushing their phone calls and was often saying she was too busy to come by after school that she was dating Dan. Instead, she found out because she just happened to come around the corner to find them face to face, Mary giggling that giggle that is only for a member of the opposite sex. The moment ended abruptly when their eyes met. Dan walked away to let them talk.

"Hi, Sarah," Mary said, unsure of herself.

Sarah glanced at Dan as he peered back over his shoulder with a cocky grin. She could only envision a lion hovering over its prey and herself, the hyena who stood on the outside with no chance of getting close to the fallen gazelle. She knew then she would only get the scraps of Mary that he didn't want, and even then, he might not be willing to share. A scream that would never be released rose inside of her. *Why, Mary, why would you walk right into this?* Sarah could only turn and walk quickly away.

"Sarah, Sarah, wait up. Please stop."

She turned on her heel. "What are you thinking? Why would you be talking to someone who turned on you so quickly like that? I'm telling you, Mary, he's bad news."

"You just have to get to know him."

"Get to know him. What are you talking about? You don't even know him."

Mary glanced at the floor. "We've been talking. He's been calling me every night. He said he wasn't the one to spread the rumors after the movies. It was Kathleen. She was only mad that I went out with him."

Mary found herself rambling on about their phone calls. The quieter Sarah became, the more Mary rambled. When she quieted, Sarah looked at her, unconvinced, before speaking.

"If he's so great, why didn't he stand up for you when the rumors were going around?"

"He's truly sorry. Please just give him a chance."

"I don't know why you didn't tell me. You've never hidden anything from me before."

"Dan just thought it was better if no one knew right now. He was trying to end things with Kathleen..."

"He was still seeing Kathleen! Mary, I don't understand you right now. You're smarter than this.

"Sarah, I really like him. I've never liked anyone like this before. Please just give him a chance."

"Whatever. Good luck. I sincerely hope Dan doesn't break your heart." Sarah walked away, leaving Mary behind her.

The phone calls had become more infrequent as Dan and Mary's relationship appeared to grow stronger. The girls seemed to avoid each other in the hallways since seeing each other seemed to bring a piercing pain to both girls, but to Sarah, it seemed like she was the only one suffering. It was the first time she ever felt alone. The hallways felt larger and longer; the quiet was more deafening, and the laughter more meaningless. She had not realized how much she had grown dependent on Mary. When she walked down the hall, she suddenly felt very aware of herself. She judged her mannerisms, her laughter, all the things that usually flowed from her naturally.

Each day passed with this discomfort until she slowly found herself speaking to new people and hearing what they were saying instead of thinking of how much she missed the comfort of her old friend. Gradually, it became less painful to see Mary as she walked hand and hand into the classroom with a boy that Sarah detested.

The lunchroom began to make her feel less exposed as she glanced out over the tables and could find a group where she could almost make herself believe she belonged. It was the place at school that told the world where everyone fits in. Students could not hide behind the assigned seating. They were able to fly, to shine with their own personality, or to crash miserably.

Sarah awkwardly slid into an already formed group of girls; Janet, Marsha, and Alice. Talking and laughing began to be exactly that, although she could not help the occasional glance over her shoulder at the newly publicized couple just to catch a glimpse of the girl she once knew so well.

She found herself surprised to see Mary coming toward her table one day. An unfamiliar hint of uncertainty replaced the sparkle in her eyes.

"Hi, Sarah. Can I sit with you today?"

"Why aren't you sitting with Dan?"

"He's getting help in math, so he's eating in the room."

"I guess so. We were just talking about what to wear to prom. Have you picked out your dress yet?"

"No. I found one, but Dan said it wasn't flattering."

"He said it wasn't flattering. When did he become a style expert?"

"He didn't think it showed off my waist."

"What? He didn't think it showed off your waist! Seriously, Mary? I can't even listen to this."

"You didn't see the dress. Anyway, I'm going to keep looking. We only have one senior prom, after all."

"We're going out shopping this weekend. Would you like to join us?" Alice tried to help, sensing the awkward tension.

"Well, I think Dan wanted to help me look."

"Why does he care so much?" Sarah snapped.

"Well, it's a big night."

"I wish you could hear yourself right now."

Sarah wanted to shake her. It was as if he had turned her into a mindless zombie in only months. She could only pray that this relationship ran its course quickly before there was nothing left of the Mary that she knew. Sarah stared in disbelief at the stranger in front of her; then she heard his voice.

"Mary, come over here."

Her head turned so quickly, like a puppet on a string.

"Dan finished up early."

"You could stay with us one day." A final plea leaped from her lips without consent.

"Mary, come on," his voice demanded.

"I better go."

"Or what?"

"Please, Sarah, don't be like that. I'll call you later."

The phone call would never come.

48

"Whatever, see you later." Sarah had not noticed how quiet everyone at her table had been until Mary got up and left.

"Forget about her, Sarah. The way Dan is, he'll dump her in the next couple of weeks, and she'll be back to normal before you know it."

"No, she'll be heartbroken." Unfortunately, there were worse possibilities than that.

MARY

Mary lay in bed, going over her day in her mind. For the first time, she saw herself through Sarah's eyes. The change in her was undeniable. She used to rule the cafeteria and was the envy of the other girls due to her style and confidence. What was happening? How was she allowing Dan to pick her dress? Fashion was something she understood more than most of her classmates. People imitated her style. Anger began to grow inside of her, and she promised herself she would be stronger.

When she later told Dan that she wanted to shop with Sarah, he slammed his locker and brought his face very close to hers. "Are you going to start doing this shit? I might as well have stayed with Kathleen. You're no different. You're either whimpering like a baby or being a bitch." He huffed by her, making sure his shoulder could push her as he passed.

Later that day, she saw Sarah at her locker, and timidly approached her.

"Hi, stranger."

"Hey."

Mary looked down at the ground, ashamed of the friend she had let herself become. "Do you hate me?"

"No, Mary, I could never hate you. I might hate Dan, though.'

"Fair enough. So, if I called you, would you hang up on me?"

"Probably not."

"I hope not. I need my friend back."

"I never left Mary. That's all on you."

"Let me start making it up to you."

"Whatever, Mary. We'll see how Dan feels about it, I guess."

That night Mary called Sarah for the first time in months. Theirs was a short conversation, but it enlivened missing energy inside of Mary, creating a need for more. The seed had been planted and was quickly taking root. She felt braver and stronger when she talked to Dan that night.

"So, are you feeling better about me shopping with the girls?"

"I don't blame you for wanting to. Listen, Mary, I didn't mean to yell at you today. It's just that sometimes I think the world wants to come between us. You know how much you mean to me. Why do you let people try to come between us?"

"I'm not letting people come between us. You hang out with your friends, friends that are, in truth, Kathleen's friends, and then you don't want me hanging out with mine. It doesn't make sense."

"I know. I know. I just love you so much. I promise I'll try to get better."

"So, I can shop with the girls this weekend?"

"I didn't say that. Who is the prom supposed to be about, you and Sarah or you and me?"

"You and me, but shopping is a girl thing. I don't know why you even want to come with me."

"Let's just say I've saved a little money and wanted to spend a bit on my girl."

"You don't have to help pay for my dress. My parents are paying for it."

"It's good practice for me. I want to take care of you for a very long time."

Mary knew his words should warm her, yet somehow, they were beginning to scorch and scar her instead. *Run. Run. Run*, is all she could hear.

"Okay, we shop for the dress, but I'm hanging out with Sarah when I feel like it."

Dan paused, and Mary could sense him steading his emotions, allowing himself time to choose his words carefully.

"Whatever makes you happy, my dear."

Mary hung up the phone. His apology fell on numb ears. Apparently, her strength frightened Dan enough to be on his best behavior for the next couple of weeks. He easily weaseled himself back into her heart, but he could not erase what lurked in her mind.

SARAH

Sarah found herself waiting for her phone to ring each night. She braced herself for disappointment, for there were still many nights that the phone remained silent. It had been several days since the last call. Mary assured her things were changing, but Dan seemed to keep her so busy that the change was hardly noticeable. Instead of feeling a reborn friendship in her future, there was only the drop of pressure before the storm. Something felt wrong.

When the phone finally rang, it was Friday night. Although it was one of the few weekends left before they graduated, Sarah was at home. Sometimes she preferred to be alone rather than spend her time with fill-in friendships. Lost in her latest novel, she heard her father's voice call to her.

"Sarah, Mary's on the phone." She raced to the living room perhaps a bit too eager.

"Hello."

"Hi, Sarah. Sorry, I took so long to call."

"That's all right." There was an awkward pause.

"What's up?"

"I was wondering if you wanted to spend the night." Mary knew better than to mention that she needed to stay home because Dan told her he would be calling after he got in from a night out with his friends.

"I guess so. I can see if my Dad can drop me off." It seemed like forever since Sarah had visited her second home. "I'll call you back in a minute." Sarah knew her father would be excited to see the two girls together again.

In a short time, she was in Mary's bedroom. Sarah glanced around the room, trying to find her place in it and noticed Mary's prom dress hanging on the closet door.

"Oh, Mary, please try it on for me."

Mary lit up as she reached for the dress and began quickly putting it on. It slid effortlessly over her shrinking frame. She tried not to think about the fact that Dan had robbed them of a moment that should have been theirs. She didn't want her opinion of the dress tainted by his involvement. Mary did a quick twirl in front of her. Sarah stared, envious of how beautiful her friend looked in her light pink dress. It was sleeveless and tapered in a way to accentuate her waistline and then flowed out in a free, careless way. She looked like a princess, so glamorous and classy.

"Mary, you look beautiful." Again, she smiled and radiated the way only Mary could.

"We never ended up shopping. I might go shopping with the girls this weekend, instead."

"I didn't miss it? I want to go with you."

"Could you? You think you'll be able to break away?" Sarah hoped she hadn't crossed the line and put Mary in defensive mode.

"I'm simply going to tell him that I'm hanging out with my best friend tomorrow, and that's that. Besides, I'm getting tired of feeling like a princess stuck in a tower anyway."

"I'm so excited, Mary!" The girls hugged tightly, laughing and imagining a day like the ones they took for granted for so many years.

"I just don't know what to do." Mary was suddenly somber and slumped her shoulders as she sat on the edge of the bed. "I love him so much, but he makes me feel trapped sometimes."

Sarah tried to choose her words wisely. "Mary, please don't be angry when I ask this, but what makes you like him so much?"

Mary hardened her gaze at Sarah. "There are things about Dan that you don't know. He only looks tough on the outside, but he struggles, too. I can't tell you everything because it's personal to him, but he's had a tough past."

Sarah let this information sink in for a minute.

"Mary, just remember, sometimes you have to think of yourself first. You can't fix everyone, you know."

Maybe Sarah was acting hypocritically. Hadn't she depended on Mary to walk beside her with enough confidence for both of them every first day of school? Hadn't Mary tutored her through calculus and chemistry? It was what Mary was good at, and Sarah loved her for it.

She knew that if Mary found an injured bird on the edge of the road, she would take it home and nurse it until it was better or dead. She would never leave the side of someone in need. Dan saw this quality in Mary, and he played the victim. Getting a glimpse into Dan's life didn't make Sarah like him more; it only made her understand his game and that Mary was his pawn. He became a child fighting demons and cried alligator tears every time he crossed the line.

For someone with so little experience with the opposite sex, Sarah knew that sometimes a person could love someone too much and not see that she could be hurting them by letting them get away with crap. Sometimes the best lesson for the sick would be to lose the things that continued to fuel them. Not that Sarah cared that much for Dan's welfare, but she feared that deep down, Mary's destruction was beginning.

"Let's forget about it for now and decide where we're going to shop tomorrow."

Mary's energy was back, and it made Sarah feel alive along with her. Just then, the phone rang, and Sarah knew it would be Dan.

"Hello."

Sarah could hear his slurred voice from where she sat, "Hey, girl. What's up?" Mary stood a bit taller before answering him.

"Sarah's staying the night. We're going shopping for her prom dress tomorrow." An eternity of silence followed her statement.

"I have plans for us tomorrow."

"Well, I'm sorry, but I am going shopping with Sarah."

"See what happens? You start hanging out with your friends, and you get all mouthy with me. You're acting like a real..."

Mary interrupted in time to cut off his obscenity. "I'll call you tomorrow. Good night." She quickly placed the phone on the receiver and took a deep breath. "Well, there you go. We're going shopping." The tower was rebuilding.

CHAPTER 6

1 9 6 7
M a r y

Sarah and Mary spent the day of prom together doing their nails, playing with hairstyles, and discussing the latest gossip. Mary only occasionally thought back to her phone call with Dan the night before when she could hear his parents arguing in the background. She was even almost successful at pushing his tender, embarrassed voice out of her head when he said he needed to get off the phone.

"So, tell me about David," Mary said.

"David's nice. I met him when I was over at Marsha's house one time, and she said he's liked me ever since."

"Oh my, Sarah. Look at the effect you have on men," Mary teased.

"Maybe you should hold your admiration until you see him. He's a bit Ichabod Cranish, but he's super nice. Plus, Marsha begged me to go on at least one date with him."

"So, you and Marsha have been pretty close?" Mary asked as she and Sarah looked at each other in the dresser mirror. Mary knelt on the bed behind her, pulling her hair into the clip that allowed the height Mary was trying to accomplish.

"Oh yeah, she's my new best friend," Mary gave Sarah's hair an extra tug.

"Ow!" The girls smiled at each other in the mirror.

"Maybe I deserved that, but it's going to get better this summer. I'm going to tell Dan that I need a little space." The feeling of fear raced through her with each word.

"Really? I mean, I'm sorry. Well, actually, I'm not, but I don't want you upset, either."

Sarah could see the look of sadness and bravery cross over her friend's face. Her chin found its proper pride position before announcing, "Don't worry about me, just start making some plans. I don't want to be bored the last summer of my youth."

"I'm already planning." Sarah thought that, just maybe, she was as radiant as her friend as a smile once suffocated, began to emerge.

The prom was a pleasant surprise. Dan kept wanting to sneak out back with his buddies to drink in the parking lot, which left Mary to be one of the girls. She seemed relieved, and Sarah noticed several times that Mary threw her head back in a real laugh. Sarah could only stop and listen to the sound she had missed so much. It was such an exuberant sound, and it made her envision how Mary was before Dan had tarnished her.

The last time Dan came stumbling in from the parking lot, he invited the girls to join them. The girls were already giddy from the night and feeling a little braver than usual, so when Dan handed them each a beer, they clinked bottles in a toast and drank up. After two, they were already feeling warm and silly. A wonderful silly. Mary grabbed Sarah's arm, and they found themselves kicking off their shoes and racing across the football field in their prom dresses and bare feet. They fell in a heap, laughing so hard that tears came to their eyes, tears caught between happiness and loss. They laid on their backs and stared up at the sky, breathing heavily from their race.

"Sarah, I hope that we're always best friends."

"Me, too." Sarah's words were more of a plea to her friend since nothing would make her wish otherwise. Dan's slurred words cut through the evening air calling Mary to him.

If only the night had ended after the prom, their whole lives would have been different. Dan's friends had planned an after-prom party. By the time they reached the party, Dan was quite drunk. Even through Sarah's blurred vision, she could see his swagger had become sloppy, and his light air had changed to something darker. He held Mary's hand in a vise, and whenever Sarah waved for her to come over to join her, Mary would simply shake her head no.

By the night's end, he seemed to be resting, maybe weeping on Mary's shoulder. She comforted herself, knowing that this may be the last time she had to share Mary with Dan, and she turned her attention to her date, who had been very patient with her throughout the night.

The only time she spoke with Mary again was to say good night. Mary's face carried the weight of a dark secret, and Sarah questioned whether she should leave her or not. The room was beginning to spin, and Sarah knew if she didn't leave the party, she could get sick in front of everyone. David gently reminded her that Mary lived right down the street and could go home anytime she wanted. Sarah glanced back at Mary. She was sure she saw fear in her eyes, but she dismissed it. That was decision one.

CHAPTER 7

Decision Two
1967
Mary

The room disappeared around Mary. She never allowed herself to drink more than one beer, and that was only a few times before. Tonight, she had lost count. She was swimming in a blur between two worlds, hers and Dan's. His world was the world she wanted to run from, yet it was quickly overtaking her. She could smell the booze as he nuzzled into her neck and knew that he had been drinking whiskey. He changed when he drank it. It allowed whatever dark that was inside him to surface.

"Mary, I've wanted to be alone with you all night. I need you right now."

She couldn't see his face as he buried it in her neck, but she thought he was crying. Mary looked one last time at her friend, laughing with her date across the room and desperately wanted to be with her. She feared the control Dan still had over her.

"Mary, I need you."

"What happened, Dan? Why are you so upset?"

"Not now."

Dan picked his head up and looked in Mary's eyes. Even with his slightly glazed look, she became lost in his sadness with him. She wondered if that's why, in the very distant past, someone created the tale of Medusa. The power of eye to eye contact could destroy. Dan turned and grabbed her beer off the table for her.

"Dan, I think I've had enough."

"Come on, Mary. You never drink with me. I mean, really drink. Just relax with me tonight."

As she was deciding, Sarah came up to say goodbye. Mary knew that Dan could walk her home from the party, so she hugged her friend goodbye. Something inside of her did not want to let go. Sarah looked back at Mary. If only she could scream, *Take me with you.* Everything was swirling. She tried to keep her focus and control. She felt Dan ease her bottle to her lips, and Mary took another long hard swallow, hoping to rid herself of the shadows that lurked around her.

For the next couple of beers, Dan was so attentive to her. He was holding her hand, or he had his hand on her back continuously. Mary was, for the first time, included in every conversation. Conversations she would barely remember in the morning. Mary wondered why he didn't always make her feel this special.

In her confused state, she decided there was no harm in the fact that she enjoyed one last night with

63

the first man she had ever loved. There was no doubt in her mind, though, that when he kissed her good night at her door, it would be their last. She took her final swallow and let Dan know it was time to go.

"It's getting late, isn't it? I put my coat in the bedroom. Come with me, and then we'll head out." He took her hand, and she innocently followed.

The coat lay on the bed exactly as Dan had said. Mary hardly noticed that he shut the door behind him when they entered the room. Everything was spinning. She felt like an observer as Dan guided her to the bed, and he sat down, still holding her hands. She stood in front of him like he was a wounded child and kissed the top of his bowed head. Naturally, her hand combed through his full head of soft hair, and then her hand grazed a large lump toward the back.

"Dan, what happened to your head?" His eyes reached up to hers, and a tear escaped down his cheek.

"Oh, Dan, tell me, please." He pulled her close, hugging her around her waist, and she could feel the gentle sobbing of his body.

"I need you so much, Mary. You're the only good in my life."

"Please tell me what happened."

"You heard him last night, didn't you? On the phone, you heard him yelling at my mom, didn't you? He was so drunk. The bastard! He was so drunk again," Dan cried. "I thought he would seriously hurt her this time. I tried to stop him. I was yelling, 'Get the fuck away from her.' All I remember is that he slammed me against the wall."

He sobbed as he somehow brought Mary down next to him on the bed. Mary rubbed the tears from his cheeks and waited for him to be able to continue.

"Mary, you're the only good in my life. I love you. You know that, don't you?"

"I love you, too."

Mary would never remember who began kissing who first. All she knew was that suddenly, she couldn't get close enough to him. Her fingers fumbled with nerves and drunkenness as she allowed them to travel over Dan's shoulders and chest being far bolder than she had ever dreamed. She was slightly aware that Dan was lifting her dress and somewhat aware that she should stop him, except everything was spinning. As he began reaching for her panties and pulling at them, the little bit of the real Mary fought to defend herself.

"Dan, I don't want to do this."

"You said you love me. I need you, Mary."

"Dan, please." She felt incredibly weak. She tried to focus, yet nothing in the room would stay still.

"Trust me, Mary."

As Mary tried to protest one more time, it was too late. She lay in shock for the moments it took for it to be over, and Dan rolled over on the bed next to her. She stared at the ceiling until she heard Dan snoring, grabbed her things, and didn't stop running until she was in her bedroom. Her parents were either fast asleep or gave her a little privacy due to prom night. Either way, they wouldn't know about her shameful moment for several months to come.

Mary would replay the night in her mind a million times. Did she start kissing him? A memory pushed forward of her drawing herself closer to him. She remembered the feeling of his muscles through his shirt and that she liked them. She remembered telling him, no; however, she didn't yell at him. She didn't push him away. A million times, she would wonder if it was her fault. A million times, she would wonder why she had allowed herself to drink so much. She called Sarah quickly the next day, laughed off a hangover, and then closed herself up in her room until she could find the confident Mary again.

SARAH—PRESENT

Sarah sat in her chair throughout the afternoon. After her programs ended, she shut the television off and enjoyed the quiet. Her breathing was the only sound that filled the air. She could see children riding their bikes past her window. It was curious to Sarah how life simply continued to go on, new people forming new memories every minute.

She wondered where those children would find themselves in sixty or seventy years. Would they still be friends, or would they barely remember each other's names? Sometimes she would ask Mary to leave the door open so the outside world could easily drift in through the screen door, but sometimes it made her feel on display.

Could these children even imagine her, a small girl, riding her bike through the streets? She knew that, to children, old age wasn't a phase of a person's life; instead, it was strictly a person trapped in this one time as if that was the only way they ever existed.

Sarah, however, knew so much had existed. Despite this, everything seemed to come down to a handful of events. Her life had become so overshadowed by the bad ones that even the good ones hurt. They were merely reminders of how much she threw away. The memories would still occasionally squeeze their way into her mind. However, through practice, she had learned to force them out as quickly as they came.

1967

Prom night. It seemed perfect. The next couple of weeks at school were about friendships, not

67

boyfriends. Dan didn't seem to mind either. There was so much excitement that filled the air. Everyone was talking about their next adventure. It was as though they were watching each other emerge from their childhood forms and into the adult they were destined to become. Some of her classmates were going off to college, while others were going right to work. Some, like Sarah, were content to wait and see. All she wanted was to be a mom and take care of her home.

No one was surprised when Mary started talking, years before graduation, about attending nursing school, and everyone knew she would be amazing. Her father's construction company was quite successful, which made it possible for them to prepare financially. Sarah knew her father would do whatever it would take to send her to school as well. She also knew this would be much more of a sacrifice for him.

Sarah fondly remembered the transition in all the parents, as well as the students. Everyone seemed to have a bit more freedom, curfews were slightly relaxed, and there was a feeling of pride in their ability to cross the imaginary line into adulthood.

Looking back, Sarah could recall signs of storms that lurked on the horizon. Despite this, she had tried to overlook them. When the group of girls ran off to go swimming in the river for the day,

Mary would only want to nap in the sun. When everyone met for milkshakes before the drive-in, Mary couldn't seem to stomach the idea. After about two months, it became painfully clear to both girls why.

When Mary finally broke down and admitted everything to Sarah, the world started to collapse around her. In an instant, the plan of ending it with Dan changed, and now they were getting married. Mary's father offered him a job with his construction company. It was apparent that since Dan's parents kicked him out of the house, he did not have a choice. Mary decided to wait a year to start nursing school, and Sarah took a job at a local diner as a waitress.

PRESENT

Maybe it was the spring air drifting into her living room that brought memories of her young self. At one point, she effortlessly hustled around tables, in and out of the kitchen, balancing trays like she was born for it. The image made her almost smile. At one time, her tired, old, heavy legs could dance through the day. The restaurant became like her very own kitchen and the customers her guests. Maybe that was why she loved that job, or perhaps it merely kept her mind busy when she so needed the distraction.

Outside she heard the screech of a small girl. The crying continued, and no one seemed to respond. Sarah grabbed the arms of her recliner and scooted toward the front of her chair. Slowly, she shifted her hands to her walker. With all her strength, Sarah lifted her body and began a slow shuffle toward the door. She pulled the storm door open and peered through the pollen-filled screen. There on the sidewalk was a girl of about eight. How she resembled Amanda so well was troubling, her daughter, now a stranger. It made her catch her breath a moment before she could speak.

"Are you okay, dear?"

The young girl stopped crying and stared into the silent house. She had passed the house a million times before, most likely, without noticing it. This time the grave of the past spoke to her. The little girl, suddenly healed, grabbed her bike and darted for her home.

Sarah's rare encounter filled her with emptiness, and she closed the door to the world, shuffled back to her seat, and let her mind drift.

CHAPTER 8
1 9 6 7
S a r a h

It was on a Wednesday, the day Sarah had the lunch shift. She slid into her pink waitress dress and thought, enjoying a momentary guilty pleasure, that this was probably the only time that her waist was thinner than Mary's. Mary still had a beautiful figure; however, Sarah could see her middle beginning to thicken. She had spoken to Mary quickly that morning before she had dashed to the bathroom with morning sickness. It made Sarah appreciate her life even though she ached for Mary. Sarah swung open the diner doors, ready to take on the world. The jingling bells announced her arrival.

"Morning, Sarah," called the cook and owner, Sam.

He was a heavy-set man that somehow managed to have a jovial, upbeat air no matter what kind of day it was outside. He could turn an angry customer into a friend within minutes. Simply being near him lifted unseen burdens.

"Morning, Sam. How was the morning crowd?"

"Oh, the usual." He came out from behind the counter with what appeared to be eggs and pancakes down the front of him. Looking down at his round belly, he was suddenly aware of how untidy he had become. "Oh my, looks like it's time for the lunch apron. You man the fort, and I'll be right back out."

Before he returned, the bells chimed three times, and Sarah was already twirling around the diner. Many customers knew her by name, which was a fact that made it seem even more like home.

She had become so lost in her world that she barely noticed her father walking in with a young man about her age. She had never met him, and she knew this because she would have remembered a face capable of making time stop.

"Hello, little lady. Do you have a seat for two available?" Her dad's smile gleamed as if he were about to bubble over with a secret.

"Hi, Daddy." She gave him a quick kiss on the cheek as she leaned in for two menus. "You can sit right over here."

"Do you remember me saying we have a new employee at the garage?"

"Umm, yeah, I guess I do."

"Well, this is Andy Turner. Andy, this is my girl, Sarah."

"Nice to meet you, Sarah."

He took her hand as if he had sealed a deal, and an electricity flowed between them that Sarah prayed she did not imagine.

"Nice to meet you too, Andy. Can I get you both some coffee?"

"That would be great."

Sarah turned to walk away and could feel his eyes on her as if it were a tangible connection between them. She got behind the counter and out of sight. Sarah needed to steady herself before emerging from her hideout. After several deep breaths, she managed to pour the coffee without spilling it.

She had never reacted the way she did that day to the mere presence of a strange man. Maybe it was the tan skin of youth slowly transforming into a man. Perhaps it was the feel of his hand taking hers, the way it wrapped around her own already claiming her. Perhaps it was her father's beaming smile of approval, which allowed her to let her guard down, or maybe all those things combined put her fate in motion, and her racing happily in its tracks.

"Have you decided what you would like?" She met his eyes, and already it felt like such a personal moment she wished her father was not observing.

"What do you recommend?"

She felt numb in his eye's embrace, and she found only a few words could spill from her mouth.

74

"The burger and fries."

"Then, I'll have a burger and fries." She smiled and turned toward the kitchen when she heard her father.

"Sarah, would you like to know what I want?" His smile was almost too broad for his face, and she wanted to crawl under the table and die.

"I'm sorry, Daddy. What would you like?"

"I'll take the burger and fries, also. You know Sarah, I was thinking that since Andy is new to the area, it might be nice if he came over for dinner one night to have a good home-cooked meal. I was telling him what a great stew you make."

"That would be nice. I'd be happy to cook a stew for you." Her words sounded silly, coming from her lips. She was so happy to be right there in that moment and couldn't wait for him to get out of the door at the same time.

"Well, then, how about Saturday night?"

"Sounds good to me," Andy agreed.

"Sounds good to me, too."

She was able to serve them their food with only a few fries toppling over onto the table and a small discrepancy on the bill that her boss later pointed out. Luckily, her father secretly paid the extra amount without drawing it to anyone's attention. She was so preoccupied with her new thoughts that she had no time to think of Mary's upcoming wedding. In only a few weeks, she would be

75

standing next to her dear friend, forcing a smile. She would be leaving Mary at the creature's lair and to an unknown future. She shook the thoughts away. Today would be spent thinking of better things.

Saturday arrived too quickly. Sarah spent the morning opening the windows, shaking out curtains that had long been collecting dust, scrubbing floors, and shining mirrors. A feeling of rebirth filled their home, a home that had become stagnant and was showing the gradual decline into complacency. The fresh summer breeze pushed out the smell of boredom and left the scent that only God himself could create, the natural smell of possibilities and renewal.

Sarah's father was working in the garage with Andy, which gave Sarah the whole day to create the atmosphere she wanted. She glanced around at her accomplishments and prepared herself for the next stage. She went to the fridge and pulled out the ingredients she would need; bacon, beef, onions mushrooms... the list went on. She started cooking the bacon that sent an aroma into the room that would battle the fresh, clean scents, eventually swirling around each other to produce the smell of a home. She began chopping and mincing, humming to herself the whole time. It was where she felt complete, being in the role of the homemaker and, hopefully someday, a mother.

Lost in thought, she was startled when she heard a gentle knock and screeching of the front door. It was the type of entrance expected from guests that did not need permission to enter.

"Hello, does my friend still live here?"

Her spine stiffened as Mary brought with her the only stress in her life.

"Well, that depends. Who's your friend?"

"I was hoping you, but since I can't seem to get through a phone conversation without getting sick, I wasn't sure."

"Oh, I don't mind. Your throwing up in my ear is a real diet incentive. I may even become a bathing suit model by the time this is over."

"You are a funny girl. Can I be your fat photographer that hides behind the lens?"

Sarah wasn't sure if joking about it was making things better or worse, but she was in too good of a mood to be serious. "Let me talk to my agent, and I'll see if I can work you in somewhere." She reached for another potato and started dicing. "So, how's the wedding planning going? Has your mom left any of it for me?"

"No chance. You would think the way my mom is going crazy over planning that she was genuinely excited. It's all about appearances with her. If she acts like it's everything that we've ever dreamed of, then it must be just that."

Sarah had to stop dicing for a moment to stare at Mary. Did she not even see the similarities between her mother and herself?

"What? Why are you looking at me like that?"

"Oh, no reason." In the moment of silence that followed, Sarah was quite sure Mary got it. "Well, you are her only child."

"Yes, that's why I have let her run with it without complaining much."

"And how are you feeling? Besides the vomiting and all."

"I'm fine. Only two weeks till the big day. The tailor called to say our dresses are in. Could you come with me on Monday for a fitting?"

"Of course." Except for small moments of silence where the weight of the world tried to nestle in, the conversation was almost normal. Mary's strength could sometimes even make Sarah believe everything would be all right.

"So is there a special occasion. I smell Murphy's Oil Soap and bacon."

Sarah had an urge to keep her excitement a secret, so she downplayed the evening. "My father's bringing home someone he works with for dinner. I told him I'd make his favorite."

"Yummy. Well, I guess I'll let you get back to it." She paused at the kitchen doorway. "Sarah, I never wanted it to be like this. I know it's been weird lately, but I need you by my side right now.

Whenever I pictured me getting married and having kids, you were always a big part of it. I know you're disappointed in me," Mary's voice cracked. Something that would seldom happen in her life, and Sarah found herself setting down her knife and going to comfort her.

"Mary, I'm not disappointed in you. I am disappointed for you. I know you wouldn't have chosen things to happen this way. I'll always be here for you. You know that."

Having Mary admit to her fears was uncomfortable for Sarah. She expected her to be the pillar of strength she needed her to be. The rawness of the moment made it impossible to look in each other's eyes, but as always, they could clearly see into each other's hearts.

Sarah heard the trucks pull into the driveway, her father leading her future to the doorstep. They were still in their work clothes and smelled of oils and sweat, a smell that was comforting to her, the smell of security and strength. Sarah, on the other hand, had scrubbed with every sweet-smelling product she could find. She was desperately hoping the scent of perfume masked the smell of Murphy's Oil Soap that had, a short time ago, soaked into her hands.

"Boy, it sure smells good in here." Andy's first words filled the home where they would linger till his last days.

"I told you my Sarah could cook."

"Thank you; dinner will be in about fifteen minutes. Could I get you a beer?" Her father was not a big drinker, but he did enjoy a cold beer and a game on television.

"That would be wonderful," Andy responded with a smile that made her weak.

The men went into the living room and began having small talk. She felt proud of herself as she showed Andy how she so easily could make a house feel like a home. It was one of the skills she had learned early, having no mother to do it for her. As her father and Andy sat in the living room watching a game, she put the final touches on dinner that included homemade rolls to go with the stew.

She was leaning over the table, setting out the silverware, and through the dim lighting of the living room, she saw Andy watching her. When she made eye contact, he didn't look away, so she tried to hold his gaze. The flush filled her face and made her giggle aloud. To cover her nervousness, she quickly went back to the stove. Her heart was racing with excitement, excitement not only about the moment, but a lifetime of possibilities.

Her focus was fading quickly, and not until the slight smell of burning reached her nose, did she remember her perfectly homemade rolls in the oven. She grabbed an oven mitt and quickly got them out. Without thinking, she set them on the white countertop. In the moment it took for her to catch her breath, the cookie sheet had permanently scarred the counter. She could only stare at the damage.

"Is everything okay in there, honey?"

She looked at the counter, at her slightly burnt rolls, and then at the two men in the living room, and she knew for absolute certain that yes, everything was okay. She cleared her throat, straightened her apron, and called the men to the table.

Sarah dished out the stew and set it in front of them so that maybe they wouldn't notice quite as much when she tried to slide her mistake in next to it. She saw Andy smirking. It was the smirk of a person that knew he was the cause of the calamity, and he appeared quite happy with himself. Her father, being a gentleman, never complained; however, Sarah noticed he stuck to two rolls versus his usual three or four. Her face never seemed to regain proper coloring, and Andy's grin lingered at the corners of his lips until the meal was over. In her father's delicate way, he led them to the next step of their relationship.

"I heard *Torn Curtain* is playing at the drive-in tonight. It sounds like something you would enjoy, Sarah."

"I've heard it's great. I'd like to see it sometime." She looked at her dad, suspiciously.

Torn Curtain was a drama, not what she would usually like at all. Andy looked from Sarah to her father and then offered up his services.

"You know, I think I would like to see that one, too. Would you mind having my company."

She tried to hold back her giddiness. "That would be fine with me. Let me take care of these dishes and freshen up."

"Freshening up sounds like a good idea. How about I run home and meet you back here in about an hour?"

Sarah tried to remain calm by pacing back and forth in her room until she heard his truck again. He came to the door wearing a pair of Levi's and a t-shirt. She could see his biceps pushing on the sleeves. She stared at him as he turned to shake hands with her father and tell him he would have her home by eleven. She tried to burn the image into her mind of the man standing before her, before her father, as he confidently prepared himself to take her on the first of endless dates. She knew beyond a doubt that she would never find another man more beautiful. He came into her life at the perfect time, as if sent to her as a personal savior. She was more thankful than words could express.

Andy opened his truck door for her and then realized that tools and gloves covered the passenger seat. As he scrambled to clear a spot, she breathed in the undeniable smell of oil lingering from his day.

Sarah felt that climbing into the cab of his truck was a leap into his world. She studied each crack in his seat, every scratch mark on his dashboard as if she were reading chapters in his life. She wanted to soak it all in, although she had no fear that she would lose it. Maybe that was part of her excitement. She knew he was hers.

The movie began and ended, but until she watched it again years later, she was unaware of the plot. She was so busy stealing glances at the man next to her that not even Paul Newman could get her attention. She didn't care that Andy knew she was studying the way the day's stubble was beginning to show through his tan skin. Not the summer tan of a lifeguard, smooth and pampered, but one that made her envision the dust and sweat of the day around his neck. She could smell his natural smell, a smell no company could bottle.

Andy turned to face her, and for a moment, they didn't move, their eyes remained locked. Sarah was aware of everything around her, yet even then, she knew the moment was too large to be contained in its own time. This moment was one that would spread out over a million memories that would cover a lifetime. Her body stayed in a warm trance as Andy leaned in and softly kissed her lips. It was not her first kiss nor her last; regardless, Sarah knew no other kiss would ever compare to it.

He smiled down at her, waking her from her girlish stupor. She giggled slightly and turned toward the rolling credits that had no meaning in her life except to bring her to that moment. The transition was as smooth as if she had simply walked across the lawn into her neighbor's grass. There were no barriers between the two worlds; they simply blended together naturally.

CHAPTER 9
1 9 6 7 - 6 8
S a r a h

Mary's wedding approached like a tsunami, sucking in all the life around it so that it would have the energy to destroy everything in its path for years to come. Sarah stood holding the flowers and watched Mary walk down the aisle with her arm locked around her father's. Mary's dress, cut loosely, hung over her slightly changing form, a form her parents refused to acknowledge outwardly. Maybe they did sense the ugliness inside of Dan, but the fear of their daughter going through a pregnancy without a husband must have conveniently blinded them. Sarah stood, watching Mary's father hand over his only daughter to a demon. She deserved so much better.

As Mary said her vows, Sarah cried. She could not muster any happiness for her friend as she envisioned the promises becoming chains, trapping Mary into a loveless marriage. She gazed out into the small group of people through her glazed eyes. Their friends from high school smiled politely at the couple. It had seemed that only moments before they were in the hallways of the church whispering rumors about the rushed wedding.

Sarah's father sat somberly, and next to him was Andy. When Sarah finally told Mary that she was bringing a date, she reacted with a mixture of bafflement and excitement.

"Sarah, I didn't know you were seeing someone. How come I didn't know that?" Mary asked. "Why wouldn't you have told me?"

"Well, it's nothing, really. He's just someone my dad introduced me to."

"Do you like him?"

She thought about it, and part of her wanted to scream, *Yes, yes, yes*, but again, something held her back.

"We've gone out a few times now, and I'm enjoying getting to know him. I was thinking of inviting him to your wedding if you don't mind."

"Of course, that's great. I can't wait to meet him. What's he look like?"

"Brown hair, brown eyes, and he has great arms." She broke off before exposing her complete obsession.

It wasn't until the reception that Sarah had an opportunity to introduce them. Sarah was too preoccupied to do anything besides slip in an occasional glance Andy's way up until then. They would share an intimate smile, one that touched each other's souls. It was a smile that tried

86

desperately to help her forget she was Maid of Honor in a wedding for a relationship that should have ended months before. Mary did care for Dan in some way, Sarah admitted to herself. Despite that, it was obligation that forced this marriage.

The reception was a small gathering in the local fire hall. Mary's mom, along with many family and friends, had prepared dishes for the guests. There was a local band, sure not to make it further than their town, and a cash bar. The wedding party entered the room when announced. Sarah walked in with Matt. Being next to him was hardly awkward since the night at the movies had meant so little to them both. They made small talk when necessary, but most of the time, they kept their distance.

Confetti danced around their heads as they walked into the party. They were the only members of the bridal party, so Mr. and Mrs. Dan Hunter were right behind them. Whenever Sarah's presence wasn't expected at the head table, she made her way over to her father and Andy, who were drinking beer and talking away about work the whole night. Finally, Mary and Dan made their rounds to the tables.

"Andy, this is Mary, and this, of course, is Dan," announced Sarah.

"Hello, Mary. Sarah talks about you a lot. It's great to finally meet you." Then he turned and shook Dan's hand.

"You have a beautiful wife. Congratulations!"

"Thank you. I'm sure we'll be seeing a lot of each other. It's hard to keep these girls apart." His words struck Sarah. Where someone else would be saying that in jest, she wondered how much effort he would put into keeping Mary from her.

"That's how good friends are, I guess," Andy replied.

"Yes, I guess that's true before they're married with a kid on the way."

Sarah swallowed the tirade of responses she was dying to give.

"Well, I think I am going to meet the best man outside for a smoke. Nice meeting you."

"Dan, you can have a smoke in here. We haven't been to all the tables."

"Oh, I'm sure they won't mind."

Mary's smile was a cover for her frustration. Anyone could see through it as if it were smoky glass. It may not fully be transparent, but one could see the shapes of her demons dancing through the haze.

"Sarah, would you come to the other tables with me?"

"Oh, sure." As they walked away, Mary grabbed her arm.

"Andy's gorgeous and so polite. I'm so happy for you, Sarah." Pride welled up inside of her.

"He's such a great guy. I'm so glad you finally got to meet him."

"Do you really like him?" She thought for a moment and could contain it no longer.

"Mary, I think I'm finally in love." Mary grabbed her and held her so tight, and only then did Sarah see her real smile.

As the night calmed down, and most of the guests were on their way home, Andy asked Sarah to go outside with him. He lit up a cigarette. She didn't know he smoked, but it was not uncommon. In fact, Sarah thought it only added a manly charm. She watched him through the gray circling wreath. His slight grin hung around the corners of his eyes as well as his lips.

"Would you like one?"

"I've never smoked before."

"Well, you don't need to for me." She stared at him wanting to share everything with him.

"Why not." She tried to imitate him, the way he held the cigarette, lit it, and breathed in the scent of it. Sarah was not nearly as smooth as him, coughing and sputtering at first as he quietly laughed.

"Well, what do you think of all this," Andy asked.

"All what?"

"This wedding stuff."

"I think it's wonderful if you're with someone you love." Butterflies swarmed in her stomach at the mere mention of marriage, even if it had nothing to do with them whatsoever.

"Well, this is not for me," Andy said.

Sarah's heart sank, hearing his words.

"You don't like marriage?"

"No, I don't like firehalls. I'd prefer an outdoor wedding, a pig roasting over a fire, cold beers that keep coming till the stars come out, very informal, you know. That's the kind of wedding a mechanic likes. What kind of wedding do you like?"

She could not help but smile at the man before her. Smoke swirled around them as if it were sealing a bond together.

"Well, it's funny that you mention that because I've always said I would never get married if there weren't a pig spinning over a fire somewhere nearby." The desire, of course, was a lie.

"Now, that is a coincidence. It sounds like I might enjoy being at your wedding." They were lost in each other's smiles until she felt his hand gently slide across her cheek, and behind her neck, drawing her in. Their lips touched, and the feeling made her numb and alive at the same time. It was only a matter of time until some pig somewhere would meet its fate.

Mary and Dan rented an apartment in town. Much to Sarah's delight, he did not try to keep them apart, mainly because he was never there. Mary's father kept him very busy at his construction company, and after work, he would often meet the other men for beers in a bar downtown. When Sarah asked Mary if this bothered her, she said she was too tired to care. Sarah didn't believe her even though she was often sick and napped more than she had ever thought possible.

As the months passed, Mary regained her energy and truly did glow. What her marriage lacked in love, her pregnancy gave her. She began talking to her belly as if her little one was already in the room with them. Then she would smile up at whoever was nearby with such radiance that the slight bit of craziness didn't matter.

Sarah was selfishly happy that Dan was so often absent because it allowed her to be such a large part of Mary's pregnancy. They watched in amazement as tiny feet pushed upon her belly or as the occasional roll showed either a head or a bottom. They were both already in love with the child. Together they shopped for a second-hand crib, and they painted the nursery a neutral yellow. Teddy bears, onesies, and pacifiers filled the room. Sarah knew that she would be throwing a baby shower for her in the next couple of months; nonetheless, neither one of them could resist.

The little person growing inside Mary consumed them both. Sarah found herself unbelievably happy that a precious baby was coming into their lives, and each time they picked out a new receiving blanket or outfit, she could see the tiny fingers of this little stranger.

It was February, and the baby was due in March. Sarah had been at Mary's mother's all day, writing out invitations and planning a brunch for the big day. When she finally made it home, she found her father and Andy sitting on the couch watching baseball and patiently waiting for dinner. Under a slight bit of annoyance in their inability to feed themselves was great pride in the fact that they needed her. She quickly put the potatoes and meatloaf in the oven and warned them it would be a late dinner.

There was something strange in the air that she could not quite understand, something secretive, despite that she never knew them to have secrets. As she busied herself setting the table, she watched them silently watching television. They weren't even making any of their usual trivial game comments.

They finally came to the table like aliens in her kitchen. Quietly, they discussed some car that would need a paint job the next day. Sarah tuned them out and cleared the table, hardly recognizing when the gears shifted.

"Sarah, why don't we go out and sit on the back porch for a bit tonight," Andy suggested.

"It's cold out there."

"We'll bring a blanket." It seemed like a strange request; however, snuggling under a blanket was beginning to interest her.

"Why don't you kids go on out there now? I'll finish cleaning up."

Hearing her father say these words sealed it. There was something distinctly strange in the air. Never, in Sarah's recent memory, had her father done dishes. She stared at them both before turning to grab a blanket. If their eyes could make a sound, they would have been giggling.

She waited beside Andy as he opened the back door for her. The chill hit her face. It wasn't freezing, nor was it comfortable. Andy pulled the rockers close and adjusted the blanket around her before saying he would be right back. She sat there looking at the stars, wrapped in her blanket, completely baffled, and then the stars disappeared behind a blinding light. She shut her eyes until they could adjust enough for her to look up again. The backyard was strung with lights, making it a landscape of glowing bushes and grass, a scene nothing short of magical.

Andy came and sat next to her, curling himself up in a blanket.

"So, what do you think?"

"It's beautiful," Sarah said. "What's it for?"

"Well, I thought we would need lights to help us cook the pig."

Things began to click, and she glanced over her shoulder into the kitchen window. She caught a glimpse of her father's head ducking out of the way, such a masculine figure in her life, slipping into such a maternal giddiness was extremely amusing to witness.

"What are you saying, Andy?"

"I believe I'm asking you to marry me."

She could only laugh and wrap her arms around his neck.

"Well, is that a yes?"

"That is definitely a yes."

She saw him reaching into his jacket pocket, and her heart began to race. Why she felt nervous was beyond her, there was nothing to be worried about with him. Andy brought out a small red velvet box and opened it for her. There was the most beautiful quarter carat that she had ever seen. Maybe that was because it was the first and only one intended for her. He slipped it on her finger and kissed her forehead. She stared at the sparkling symbol of promise on her finger until tears blurred her vision.

1968

Sarah planned her wedding for July, allowing Mary time to recover from childbirth and fit into her Maid of Honor dress. Andy's best man was his brother, Collin. Sarah would only meet him a few times before the wedding, just like his parents, Phil and Laura Turner. When Andy told them he was getting married, they drove the twelve hours to meet their daughter-in-law. It was a meeting that Mary helped her through successfully. Mary's natural ease with people calmed Sarah's nerves, and soon she was able to enjoy finding out everything she could about Andy as a young boy.

His mother brought photo albums and memories galore. She shared everything through a few tears. Sarah found herself quickly falling in love with the whole family, and she wondered how Andy could ever leave them. Unfortunately, the distance would prevent them from forming the bonds that Sarah would have enjoyed.

Andy had grown up in a small town in New York and went to work in his father's garage as soon as he could lift a wrench. He wasn't put on the payroll until much after that. His life was mostly happy, as well as typical. His brother was already off at college when Andy graduated from high school, and the town felt too small without him. Andy needed an adventure, and college was not in his plans. When his father needed a car driven to Virginia, Andy jumped at the chance and drove right into Sarah's life. He pulled into her father's garage, saw the help wanted sign and destiny, took over. His family would occasionally visit through the years; however, their relationship consisted mostly of phone calls and letters.

Between the shower, planning the wedding, and of course, the big day, the birth of Mary's baby, the girls had no time to worry about Dan and what he was or was not doing. It was a needed relief for them both.

Mary went with Sarah to try on wedding dresses. Sarah was on about her fourth one, not dissatisfied with any of them, yet enjoying being a princess too much to stop the fashion show. She came out of the fitting room, twirling. When the room settled, her eyes focused on Mary's face. Her smile had disappeared and left only a ghostly white replica of her friend.

"What's wrong?"

"My water broke."

Sarah quickly became the nervous husband forgetting how to undo her zipper, tripping over dresses, and putting her shirt on backward. She raced to the phone and dialed Dan's work to let him know. He was out on some truck somewhere, and they would locate him. Arm in arm, they got to the car, and she drove her to the hospital.

Sarah and Mary's parents paced around the waiting room. Andy eventually came to wait with them, and Sarah selfishly let her mind start to picture Andy waiting for her. She couldn't wait to be experiencing the birth of their child.

It was Andy that asked where Dan was. Sarah stopped pacing, frustrated with the mention of Dan's name as if his absence was unimportant. Despite her internal struggle, Sarah pushed the selfish thought from her mind. Mary shouldn't have to depend solely on her friends.

"We've called him several times," Sarah said, "but we haven't got a hold of him."

Andy headed to the lobby where the only payphone was located, a look of disgust on his face. The exchange of glances continued to progress as each phone call came up empty. After many attempts, Andy returned, clearly frustrated.

"No luck?" Sarah asked.

"He's out celebrating."

Sarah saw Mary's father slightly shake his head. Beyond that simple reaction, both parents kept their opinions well hidden. Then it happened. A tiny perfect little girl named Karen entered their lives. The nurse announced her arrival, and the room let out a sigh of excitement and relief. Sarah looked around the waiting room, and she knew Karen would never lack for love despite her father.

Eventually, the nurses allowed them to see Mary. They watched the baby in awe; however, they could only ignore the fact that Dan wasn't coming for so long. Mary sat, sweaty and exhausted, holding Karen; her smile never faded when she spoke.

"So, where is he?"

Sarah looked up at Mary's mother for guidance. She shrugged as if to say, *You have to tell her.*

"He went out to celebrate with some friends."

After a moment, Mary responded.

"Well, I guess that's what men get to do on the day of the birth."

Sarah studied her friend, her sweat drenched hair sticking to her face. Mary was the strongest woman she knew. Dan's inappropriate choices would never be okay. Despite this, Mary needed them to believe she would be okay, that she could brush off anything and still be standing. Sarah smiled at her friend, wanting to believe her, despite knowing that no one could pretend forever.

When Mary and Sarah weren't doting on Karen, Mary's mother was. That allowed them time to plan Sarah's wedding. They planted black-eyed Susans in Sarah's garden earlier in the spring to use in the bouquets. They talked to the firefighters to get a loan on tables and chairs, and they "hunted" for a pig. Sarah decided to use the same band that Mary did since the selection was so limited. Mary's mom agreed to help them make side dishes for the fifty people that would fill their backyard while the men took care of the alcohol.

The summer flew by, and the day became a reality. They restrung the lights, carefully placed the flower bouquets on the tables, and had the pig spinning slowly throughout the day. Everything was perfect. The sun shone down on them, and the humidity took a day off. The two women stood in the kitchen, waiting for the wedding march to begin. Mary tucked in a strand of Sarah's hair that was starting to fall. It seemed fitting that Mary, the one that had taught Sarah all her beauty secrets, was also her hairdresser for her wedding.

"Did you fix it?"

"Yes, you look so beautiful."

"Thanks to you."

"It has nothing to do with me." They smiled quietly at each other.

"Look at us, all grown up. It seemed to happen overnight, didn't it? One minute we were selling lemonade, and the next, we're walking down the aisle."

"You're right about that." Mary adjusted another strand of Sarah's hair. "You never know, maybe the best is yet to come."

"I believe it is."

The wedding march began, and Mary gave her friend a quick hug before turning for the door. Sarah's father came and took her arm, and they followed Mary down the grassy aisle. She didn't know then how special it would be in her life that she got married in her backyard. She didn't know how many nights she and Andy would spend staring out over that very yard, watching their children play, talking about their days, or just silently soaking in the night.

She stepped off the back porch and walked slowly toward Andy; toward the beginning of their married life together, and all the happiness she knew they would bring each other. She drank in the sound of his voice pledging his love to her and hoped her voice sounded as angelic to him. They turned toward the crowd as Mr. and Mrs. Turner. Champagne corks shot up to the heavens, and the scent of roasted pig filled the air.

CHAPTER 10

1 9 6 9 - 1 9 7 1
S a r a h

Homes of many styles lined Sarah's street; only a few were newly built. Some houses stood freshly painted by young families announcing their new beginning. Some were well-manicured and spoiled, representing the established families with money and knowledge, and some were dilapidated and worn unable to keep up with the inclement weather and time that passed. The few homes that became vacant began to fall apart quickly.

It was as though the houses themselves sensed there was no more need for them, and they started their descent back to the ground from where they seemed to have sprung. The wood would eventually become soil. The metals would grow moss and masquerade as natural surroundings, leaving only brick chimneys that would stand like gravestones as a reminder that they once existed. Maybe people could also sense when their job was complete.

After Andy and Sarah were married, he moved into their home with Sarah and her father. A situation intended to be temporary; however, destiny had other plans. Sarah's father was still a young man in his fifties. His tall frame was always a beacon in Sarah's life, pointing her in the right direction, and she believed she was a good follower. Her trust in him made it easy not to question or stray far from his protective guidance. Now, as Andy's wife, she found this was guidance she no longer often needed. She was like a comet shot through space on a specific path, and unless something knocked her out of her orbit, she would remain steady.

Sarah stood in the kitchen, completing dinner. Her roasting chicken sizzled in the oven as the natural juices helped to turn the skin to a crispy golden brown. It stood in its pan as a centerpiece to the onions, carrots, and potatoes. Sarah glanced into the living room. Usually, the picture of Andy and her father brought her peace. Now, the image before her caused her to stop short. Her father looked ashen. The summer glow had barely had time to fade, and the grayish color had no place on his stoic face. She filled a glass of water and brought it to him.

"Hey, Daddy, are you feeling all right?"

"Oh, I'm just a bit tired. I may need to go in and lay down actually." Andy looked up from the television at this point, having been oblivious to her father's condition.

"Want some help into the bedroom, Jay?"

"I'm not that old yet." He stood slowly and made his way to the bedroom turning at the doorway. "If I fall asleep, don't wake me for dinner."

"Okay, Daddy. Are you sure you're okay?"

"I need some rest, honey. I'll be fine."

Her father would never walk from the room again. The doctor said he died painlessly in his sleep from a heart attack. He made sure that she had someone to look after her, a home to live in, and countless beautiful memories to keep with her. Only then did he go to his resting place.

Many people attended the funeral. People that Sarah knew well and people that she could not remember meeting. She looked around the funeral parlor and felt honored to call such a beloved man her father. She knew that no one in the room could say a bad thing about him.

Mary stayed with her the entire service, holding her hand when needed. Sarah knew Mary must be suffering too, for her father had been so dear to her as well. In the back of the room, Sarah saw Dan talking with a woman that she had seen around town. A red flag went up, but Sarah couldn't explain to herself why. Maybe it was because she simply disliked him so much. She decided not to dwell on it and returned her attention to the guests.

Andy received ownership of her father's garage, and Sarah continued to make their house a home. Her father had left her with a feeling of peace and security in who she was. Blindly, she expected that feeling would last her for the rest of her days. She didn't know then that she would eventually stop listening to his whispers from the grave, and in doing so, risk the loss of all things she held most important; family, friends, and her very soul.

Mary gave the honor of Karen's unofficial godparents to Sarah and Andy. Sarah thought it interesting since Mary never claimed to be religious. Mary explained that she wouldn't be any good at teaching Karen the spiritual side of things and thought maybe it would be best for Karen, and any future children, to be exposed to many different beliefs.

When Karen was six months old, Mary announced she was going to begin the nursing program. Sarah jumped at the chance to babysit. She was eager to start a family of her own, but after months of trying, there was no success. Her home quickly became filled with all the baby essentials and many nonessentials as well. Week after week, Karen came into their home, and Sarah took pride in the fact that she was becoming a second mother. She adored Karen and looked forward to her curly blond hair, pink ribbon, and all, coming through her door each morning. The weeks easily became months, and too quickly, a year had passed.

When Mary came to Sarah, excited with the announcement of her second child, Sarah felt a small punch to her femininity. Mary, of course, would have never wanted her to feel that way; nevertheless, she did. Each time Sarah got to feel the baby kick, it made her ache, and each time Mary rubbed her growing belly, she felt her own hand reach down to her flat, barren one. Sarah was able to spend so much time with Mary during her pregnancies. She suspected it was because Dan had no interest in a growing belly, and it was during this time Sarah began to hear the first rumors and to see the first glances of secrecy.

Mary and Sarah went to their small grocery store to buy diapers and other necessities. They were standing in aisle nine, comparing prices when Kathleen came across their path. She prepared herself for pleasantries and then noticed how Kathleen turned on her heel to go in the other direction before Mary even saw her. Sarah could not help but watch where Kathleen so quickly headed. She approached a woman that Sarah did not recognize and whispered in her ear. They both glanced toward Mary, noticed Sarah looking, and headed for the door. It was a moment that body language screamed trouble.

"So, should I save the dollar and go for the cheaper brand, or will I be scrubbing sheets tomorrow?"

"Umm, save the dollar and try them once."

"Good call. I'll bring you the laundry."

Sarah was too distracted to laugh at her joke. She knew that Dan was doing something. She couldn't tell if it was flirting, or something much more involved, but something was going on. Sarah could not imagine Andy becoming repulsed by her growing belly and running to someone else, then again, Andy had never been like Dan.

As much as she disliked her friend's husband, she was beginning to accept him and even be grateful he chose to go out after work rather than home. The less influence he had in their lives, the better off they were in her opinion. He could just be a paycheck from another state as far as she was concerned, but now everything had changed. Her insides clenched as if she was the one Dan was betraying.

Andy came home from work and forgivingly picked up the stuffed animals, rattles, and blankets that Sarah had sprawled across the floor during Mary's visit. She watched and thanked God for the dear man that he was and pictured the father he would be. When he reached her, he took her face in his hands and kissed her in a powerful yet tender way, a way that said you belong to me, and I treasure you. It was always how she felt with him. He immediately saw the sadness in her eyes and asked her about it. Not being able to keep anything from him, she spilled her worries.

"Now, Sarah, don't jump to conclusions."

"I agree," Sarah said, "but what would you think if you saw that? Kathleen and Mary didn't leave high school on bad terms. They had resolved their differences, and Kathleen seemed to understand there wasn't a place for her now. Why would she have acted so funny after all this time?"

"I don't know, Sarah. I hope that you're wrong, but until you have more proof than a strange look and some whispers, I would leave it alone. She's expecting a child and doesn't need any stress like that."

"You're right." Sarah was quiet a moment. "Will you promise to tell me if you hear anything going on?"

Andy appeared to ponder the question, which she didn't take as a good sign. "I can't promise. I will say I haven't heard anything concrete; however, if his name comes up, there's usually an understanding."

"What do you mean, understanding?"

"He isn't the greatest character. I just don't know if I would want to put you in a position to deal with that."

"Of course, I would want to deal with it. I would want to know."

"Sometimes, things are better off not being talked about."

"How can you say that? If he's cheating on Mary, then she should know! It sounds like you think it's okay if he does."

"You know me better than that, and don't ever group me with him!" Andy paused. "Sarah, she has a baby and another on the way. She has no job, no money. What would she do? Maybe this isn't the time. Maybe being blind for a while is better."

"I can't even talk about this. I feel sick."

"Then let's not talk about it. Actually, let's start over." Andy grasped her face, kissed her softly, and looked her in the eyes. "I love you, Sarah. Now let's eat." He gently slapped her backside and turned toward the table. Taking a deep breath, Sarah shoved the day's events to the back parts of her mind, the place designed for problems that don't have solutions.

That night, they lay together content and warm in each other's arms. Outside their walls there swirled a terrible storm, but in their room, they lay innocently thinking they were safely out of its path. Unfortunately, there is always a small crack somewhere that will let the chilling winds in, and there are no blankets thick enough to keep it away once it's inside.

The for sale sign went up across the street from Sarah's house when Mary was about six months pregnant. Sarah went out to greet her when she drove up. She was bent over, getting Karen out of the car while struggling to lift her large belly with her skinny legs and chuckling at herself through the struggle. They both ended up staring at the sign at the same time and then at each other.

"Mary, you have got to buy it."

"Oh my gosh, Sarah. Can you imagine? It would be so wonderful. We could have coffee every morning. Our kids could play." She paused, "You'll have them when the time is right. I'm so excited. I can't wait to talk to Dan."

"It's a cute house, too. It has the cutest room for a nursery. Oh, I hope it works. What do you think Dan will say?" For a second, darkness clouded her eyes.

"I'll work on him."

A couple of months later, they were moving in across the street. Sarah could only believe it was the fact that he wanted her quiet and happy so he could continue living his bachelor lifestyle without complaints from her. It worked, too. She was almost a single mother through her years of pregnancy and nursing. Sarah wondered what they were like together now that they were parents. Did they ever act romantic? Did they even really love each other?

This time, when Mary went into labor, it was the middle of the night. Sarah became Karen's babysitter, and Dan drove her to the hospital. She sat up all night, wishing she could be there with her and hoped all was going well. About seven in the morning, Mary's mother called her and told her that Mary had another little girl, completely perfect. They named her Eva.

Except for the undisputable shortcomings of Dan as both a father and a husband, time passed peacefully. When Karen was two-years-old, Sarah was still not pregnant, and Mary landed her first nursing job. Sarah happily took on another child, still hoping for her own.

When Eva was about two, Dan started to be around more; however, he was miserable. Sarah could tell something must have gone wrong in his other life, so he was going to make everyone in this one suffer along with him. If she planned on taking the girls to the park in the afternoon, he would show up and say he had decided to have lunch with his girls. They would run to him so excited, believing their "loving" father wanted to spend time with them.

Sarah always tried to put a good face on for the girls. Instead of showing her irritation, she politely said, "Well, we were just heading to the park." Sarah tried to unclench her teeth before continuing. "But, I'm sure they would prefer time with their father."

His smile faded as his face turned toward her, and he said, "Yes, they would. You probably don't

get that since you don't have children of your own."
His words were daggers that pierced her heart. It
wasn't the words as much as the force behind them
that pained her. His attempt at playing father wasn't
about his love for his children; it was about control.
She could only watch as he carried them out the
door, a fake smile spread across his face.

MARY
1971

Mary sat slumped at her vanity chair, looking
at a person she could not even recognize. It was rare
for her to let herself think about her life. The times
were even more isolated now that she was working
full-time and raising a two and four-year-old. She
thought of her daughters at the park with Dan. The
very idea confused her. He was, for the most part,
an absentee parent to his girls. Despite this, or
maybe due to the fact, the minute he showed any
interest, they ran to him, hungry for attention.

Mary would bet all she had that Dan gave his
attention to the girls for all the wrong reasons. He
used them to make her angry, to show his control
and power over everything. She knew, though, that
if she felt they were in danger, she could leave in a
heartbeat, but they weren't. She would smile at
them when they walked in the door and ask them
how their time was with Daddy, and they would tell

her about all the cool things they saw, and she would act happy for them. That's what she did, she pretended, and Mary knew she was being forced to fake her way through life way too often.

After Eva was born and after she got her figure back, Dan started to show interest again. However, the attention he was giving was worse than the complete avoidance she had withstood for the years she had spent pregnant and nursing. When she looked in his eyes, all she saw was anger. It was the same anger she saw when he was on the football field years before, an eternity ago. Now the anger was directed at her. Whenever they were intimate, she felt more like an object shoved to the side after he finished with her. Would she ever know tenderness? Would she ever really know what it felt like to be loved?

She remembered how easily Dan had made her so weak and so subservient in high school, and she refused to let it happen again. The glimmer of hope she had for saving Dan from his anger had long subsided. She knew it was time to start protecting herself and her children, and she was determined to let him know, too.

Mary began locking the bedroom door when she knew he would be stumbling in too drunk to speak but not too drunk to use her again. She would lay in bed, waiting for a reaction that she was sure would frighten her. The kitchen door opened and shut. The chair screeched across the floor as Mary envisioned him pulling it out before sitting to remove his boots. Then she heard his footsteps on the stairs.

She pulled the covers to her chin like a defenseless child and tried to breathe evenly. The doorknob wiggled unproductively, and then there was silence. One loud slam against the door announced his power, and then Mary heard him shuffling back down the stairs. Dan stopped coming up the stairs on those nights. Something else clouded the relief that tried to wash over her, something that every wife surely dreads, the feeling of abandonment. She would have never guessed how easy it would be for him to stay away.

CHAPTER 11
1972-1975
Sarah

And then it happened. Sarah woke up and ran to the bathroom. The waves of nausea rolled through her like a spring storm chasing away the winter. Despite the fact she was sitting on her bathroom floor, feeling worse than she had in a long time, a smile spread across her face. Her cycle was late. She had refused to get her hopes up, but now, she couldn't help herself. As the feelings passed, she was able to jump in the shower and prepare herself for her day of babysitting. She had no fear of not being able to handle her impending lack of energy and occasional sickness. She embraced every inconvenience picturing the tiny being inside of her.

As she finished pinning up her hair, the familiar knock and simultaneous opening of the door was followed by the voices of Mary and the girls. The little feet padded across the room to the toybox in the corner, even they sounded better than they had ever sounded before. Mary stood at the door, unpacking diaper bags and extra baby food.

Her figure was back to that of a teenager, and, as always, she glowed. If her husband was mean, she found happiness with her children. If the day were rainy, Mary would find happiness in a hobby or being lazy with her girls. Sarah wondered where her internal beam came from and why everyone couldn't see the world that Mary did. Today, Sarah radiated as well. She stood watching her friend unpack and listened to words she did not comprehend, directions of some sort that she would figure out later. When Mary finally glanced Sarah's way, a face half-crazed with excitement, stared back. Mary froze.

"Sarah, please tell me that look is what I think it is."

"Well, what do you think it is?" Her eyes danced in a giggle.

Mary screamed, startling Eva, who ran to her leg and clung to it. She hobbled toward Sarah, toddler in tow, and they squeezed each other, squealing together.

"Oh, my Lord. Andy must be so happy."

"Well, actually, I haven't told him yet," Sarah said. "I haven't got an official confirmation, but I know. Don't say a word until I speak to the doctor."

"I won't, I promise. Oh darn, I have to go, or I'll be late. I'm so excited for you," Mary exclaimed. "I'm not even gonna be able to focus today. I'll be thinking of nursery colors, and oh, I'll have to get my maternity clothes, and..."

"Mary, get going. Let me talk to the doctor before you start slipping me into elastic waistbands." Sarah's mind was racing through Mary's wardrobe, silently dressing her growing belly in all her favorite outfits.

She was lucky to get in to see the doctor that day and left Mary's children with her mother. Her confidence dwindled as she sat waiting for the results. Feelings of doubt crept into her mind as she pictured herself crawling back to Mary with her humiliating news. She mentally studied every sensation in her stomach, every churn, searching for another feeling of sickness. There was nothing. Then came the light knock, and the door began to open.

She attempted to read the results by studying Dr. Snell's expression. Her face remained lowered as she reviewed the paperwork, making it impossible to read. Sarah's heart pounded in her ears; her dreams wavered on the words that would come from the doctor's mouth. As if in slow motion, the doctor's head lifted, and her lips parted to form a smile followed by the word congratulations. She was not quite sure how many hugs gynecologists received daily, but Sarah jumped from the table, wrapped her arms around her, and thanked her as if she had created her child herself.

That night there would be steak for dinner, the best ribeye the butcher could find. Andy's favorite meal, it was a meal saved for birthdays and Valentine's since it was not conducive to Andy's budget. Sarah bought a bottle of wine that she hoped was a good one, potatoes, asparagus, and French bread that she would broil to the perfect garlicky, buttery crispness on the outside while soft and warm on the inside. She found the candles buried in the bottom drawer of the buffet and set them in the center of the table.

It was perfect. Everything felt perfect. Except for the smell of beef that became irritating to her stomach, and then sped up to be completely unbearable. She dashed to the bathroom. Her hair, once pinned up perfectly, tumbled in front of her face. The red lipstick was wiped clean away by the cloth she grasped in her hand. The front door creaked open at the same time another wave sent her heaving into the porcelain bowl.

"Sarah! Sarah! Are you all right?"

"Yes," she found her voice. "Could you check the steaks?"

Sarah heard him heading in the kitchen and shutting off the burner.

"Steaks? Did I forget an anniversary or…"

Everything went silent. She could picture him staring at the table, romantically set, putting the puzzle pieces together. She heard his footsteps

117

cautiously come into the bathroom. For a man that always tried to make her feel like whatever happened with children was fine with him, he was without words. He came down on his knees and studied her frazzled face.

"Sarah, is this what I think?"

"This is exactly what you think." Andy wrapped her in his arms and simply held her for what seemed like a long time. She believed it was to hide the tears in his eyes, and she allowed him his private moment.

The maternity clothes appeared on her doorstep the next morning while she was out for a walk. She dragged the garbage bag to her bedroom and took turns holding each garment up to herself in the full-length mirror. She was months away from each band of elastic. She could hear Andy mowing the grass outside, the same lawn that her father once mowed, and someday maybe a son.

"Hello, has anyone seen a bag of maternity clothes. They seem to have been stolen from my house." The screen door slammed shut behind Mary.

"I haven't seen a thing, but really, when did you ever fit in this bra?" Sarah held up the D cup to her barely B's.

"Your time is coming, my friend; your time is coming." Mary rounded the corner into her room, her bright smile making an already perfect day better.

"I can't imagine Andy. What will Andy do with them? He'll think he's having a fling with Dolly Parton."

Mary lifted one of her favorites. Sarah remembered seeing her in it often, black slacks and a pink top that somehow made the passerby envious of her figure even when she was nine months along.

"I'll never wear this again."

"You never know, maybe you will have another."

"No, Dan is pretty adamant about that." A million thoughts passed between them.

"How many children would you like?"

"Truly, now that I'm working, it would be hard to have more, but part of me thinks I could handle a houseful. Maybe that's because my girls are at your house half the time." They both laughed as they continued rummaging through the heap of clothes.

"You could always get a job on the children's floor."

"Way too depressing. I like the emergency room. There's always a new story coming in," Mary said. "You never know what you will find each shift. Do you ever think of doing something outside the home?"

"I was starting to think I would have to, but with a baby on the way...well, it's really all I've ever wanted to do is be a mom in this house." A smile spread across her face. "This is truly everything I've ever wanted."

Mary was running her hand over a purple maternity top that had a thin tie running around the back.

"Do you feel like you have what you wanted, Mary?"

"Almost. I have two beautiful girls, the very best friend I could ask for, a cute little house across the road from her, and a husband who supports us. It sounds great when I put it that way, doesn't it?"

"Yeah, it does." Mary sat on the bed, looking somehow crumpled in spirit. Sarah laid the outfit she was holding down and went to join her.

"You know, you can always talk to me." Mary's head rested on her shoulder.

"I guess most pictures have their flaws."

Sarah waited for more, but that was all she needed to say.

Amanda came into the world in the middle of the night. Andy called Mary when they reached the hospital. She had always promised to be there, but at midnight, Dan still wasn't home. One o'clock came, and he still was nowhere to be found. By three, Amanda was in Sarah's arms. Daddy sat tenderly, touching Amanda's fingers, soaking in the long fingernails and soft brown hair barely covering her slightly cone-shaped head. By five, they had her in the nursery so Sarah could sleep, and by nine she was awoken to Mary coming in the door. Her perfectly styled hair could not distract Sarah from her puffy eyes. Despite Mary's noticeable effort, no amount of make-up could cover the wreckage left behind after a heart-wrenching cry.

"Mary, are you all right?"

"Sarah, don't you dare try to talk about me right now. Tell me all about the baby."

Sarah stared into eyes that were drowning in sadness, her smile so forced. Sarah knew she would not speak of it until later, so she let it go.

"Well, it was worse than you told me it would be, and then it was better than I could have ever imagined. Did you go see Amanda?"

"No, not yet. I wanted to see you first. I was hoping to catch you both in here."

"I'll call for the nurse. Wait till you see her. She's perfect."

Within minutes the nurse wheeled Amanda into the room, and she was swept into Mary's arms immediately.

"Oh, Sarah, she is perfect."

Mary found a chair and sat silently, studying her little fingers and toes that had to be wrestled gently from inside the cocoon they had wrapped her in.

"So, what time did he get home?"

"We don't need to talk about that right now." Sarah had decided they had waited long enough.

"Don't hold back for me. I want to know."

"I think it was around four. I fell asleep waiting sometime after three. He stumbled around the kitchen, broke a glass, and threw up on my bathroom floor. Which, of course, I had to clean up because he was too sick to do it himself. I had to take the girls to my mother's so that I could come by here. I told my mom he was working." She stood and brought Amanda to Sarah. She could see her eyes glistening from tears that she would not let fall. "It's just embarrassing."

"Why would you be embarrassed? He's the one acting like he never graduated from high school."

She went over and had a seat in the chair again. Her gaze went to the window where a parking lot blotted with a few flowering trees held her attention.

"Sometimes, I don't even care if he comes home."

Her voice was so low Sarah was not quite sure she understood her correctly.

"Mary, why don't you leave him?"

"Because I know you don't believe this, but I have more control this way. If I left him, he would take the kids all the time just to piss me off. It's better this way. He still pisses me off, but the kids will never have to be children that went through a divorce, and besides, the rare times he pretends to care are important for the girls. Eventually, when the time is right, it will all work out."

Sarah couldn't argue. Their conversation on that day would be one to set the tone for the future. They would continue not to rock the boat and hope that, with time, Dan would disappear on his own once the children were old enough not to care.

Mary's hand went up to stop her from saying anything else.

"I can't believe we're talking about this when you just had your baby. No more talk about ugly stuff. Tell me how Andy was."

Sarah smiled at her friend, amazed by her strength, before sharing every detail of the best moment of her life.

MARY

What Mary would not tell Sarah was that she was hearing the rumors that were beginning to move like an innocent butterfly around the town, eagerly landing on each permissive ear to spread her disgrace. Whispers in the grocery stores, looks on the streets, suspicions that days later turned into reality when she addressed her mother. Mrs. Allen was always a strong woman who learned early to turn the other cheek. She knew it was time to teach her daughter how to hold her head high, no matter what life brought her.

Her mother stoically confessed to Mary that Kathleen had been picking Dan up for lunch. Mary listened to words not intended to wound, yet every syllable willed her tears to betray her. She swallowed once and then forced the feelings to subside and give way to something else, something she could live with, relief. Mary let him go. As she looked at her mother across her kitchen table, she let Dan become something other than a husband to her. She would put in her time for the children, and then she would... she would keep breathing.

It would be only two years before Mary got to hold Sarah's hand through the birth of her second child. Andy paced back and forth in the waiting room until Mary came out to tell him he had a little boy. In one arm, Dan held a sleeping toddler drooling down his slightly oil-stained shirt. In the other arm, he held his son's first gift, a baseball mitt that wouldn't fit him for years. No technology could tell him the sex of the baby, yet somehow, he knew, and the acknowledgment wrapped around him, making him complete.

CHAPTER 12
1979-1986
Sarah

*T*he *Lawrence Welk Show* was about to end as Sarah sat brushing out Amanda's long brown hair. Stroke after stroke, she watched it gleam in the small lamp's light. She was six and still so innocent of all the bad in the world. Sarah prided herself in protecting her children from the darkness in the world. She wanted to be the parent her father was to her, but she didn't need to do it alone. Together, she and Andy created a warmth that seeped through the cracks of her aging house, the small dings so loyally polished that the years were hardly noticeable.

Across the street, Mary served as an extension of this warmth. If one of them needed a break from the stresses of motherhood, the other would take all four of the children. A short walk to the park, or a drive to the local ice cream stand, would allow the frazzled parent just enough time to miss their children's smiles.

For Sarah, her solace was so easily found watching her family through the window to the backyard. The sounds of laughter and their tiny voices giggling through the word Daddy would reach her through the polished glass. Sometimes there were no words, but she could see the back of their heads as they sat curled up under a blanket. One child snuggled in each of Andy's arms as they shared whispered stories that only the stars could hear. Sarah would find herself frozen in her task; the dish towel left to dangle as the world stopped a moment. A moment long enough for Sarah to again give thanks to God for never leaving her side.

Fall was closing in, and the air had begun to shift. The coolness that followed should have warned them that sometimes God watches us from behind the clouds. Mary and Sarah loaded picnic baskets, blankets, and bats and balls to head to the park. Luckily, Mary's girls were at the age to find Kyle adorable and would spend hours tossing the ball to his miniature bat until they were lucky enough to contact it. Then one of them would chase him as he giggled too hard to see the baselines. Eventually he would find home plate and declare victory. Sarah and Mary would sit and watch while catching up on the neighborhood gossip.

For weeks, some of the women in town had become obsessed with stories of being watched. Eerie feelings that lingered from the bushes when they carried in groceries or watched television at night. Mary and Sarah would privately roll their eyes at the desperate women attempting to find excitement in a quiet small town by creating ghost stories. In the stagnant air, even fear felt like something to them. Sarah would politely listen, knowing that she could remain happy with the predictability that others found monotonous.

Sarah and Mary could see the women already engaged in a deep conversation. Beverly, the flirt of the neighborhood, was clearly upset. Carol, who lived in Beverly's shadow, rubbed her back, trying to console her. Sarah glanced around the small park for another bench. She did so even though an unwritten law demanded that she join in the drama yet again.

"Good morning, ladies," Mary broke in.

Both women looked up with a new level of desperation in their eyes. Sarah did a private sigh to prepare herself.

Carol began, "Someone was watching Beverly through her window last night.

"Again?" Mary's response dripped with something between sympathy and annoyance. An eye roll passed between the friends making her true feelings clear. "We're going to have to get a neighborhood watch and catch this guy in action. All these feelings without proof for the police to go on. Very frustrating." Sarah elbowed her slightly, letting Mary know the sarcasm was evident.

"That's the thing. This time there is proof."

Sarah felt an internal chuckle, and it took extra force to swallow it down before speaking.

"What proof do we have?" she asked.

"Go ahead. You tell them. I simply can't repeat it," mumbled Beverly behind her tissue.

Carol gave her back one more rub before she removed her hand to position herself as one might for storytelling effect.

"Last night, Beverly kept feeling like someone was watching her. You know, like we've been saying. Just this feeling like you're not alone. She tried to tell herself that she was only being silly but decided she would shut her blinds anyway. When she stood up, she noticed her dog. You know Rusty; he's the most passive thing in the world. Well, she notices that he is staring at the window." Carol looked from Mary to Sarah, possibly gauging if she needed to insert more drama in her voice. "Of course, this gave her the creeps. As she walked up to shut the blinds, Rusty starts growling at the window. She raced up to it and swung the curtain shut and then ran to call Bill. He was down at the tavern. He raced home."

"I tried to tell myself that I was only paranoid. I truly did," Beverly insisted.

"Well, Bill races home, grabs some flashlights, and goes looking around the house. Right next to the window, there were footprints. Someone had been watching her from outside her window."

Sarah and Mary stood in silence. Both of their minds were struggling to find a way to laugh off her ridiculous story. Instead, they both felt it deep in their souls. Things were changing.

It was days later that Mary called to inform Sarah of yet another story. Shirley, a widow on the other side of town, had reported a peeping Tom. According to the neighborhood gossip, she was watching television just as Beverly had been when she thought she saw something move by her window. When Shirley stood to check it out, she heard a crash and could see something had knocked over her garbage can. In the morning, she walked the perimeter of the house and found footprints approaching her window that appeared to be made by work boots.

Trying to stay quiet so her children would not be curious about her conversation, Sarah whispered into the phone, "Well, that's interesting. Listen, I'll call you in the morning, and we'll talk more."

"Good night, Sarah. Maybe we should close our blinds when we watch television at night."

"I agree. Better safe than sorry. Call me if you need me." She laid the phone back in the cradle.

The bubbles began to fall, signaling the end of *The Lawrence Welk Show*. She was amazed it still captured her children's attention. Sarah hugged them each a little tighter that night before double-checking that the blinds were closed tightly. She would never know that Andy woke many times to pace by the windows like a soldier in the night, peering into the darkness, ready to ward off the evil.

Weeks passed before another woman was carrying in her groceries after a late shift at work. Her husband sat inside the house, lost in his television program. A sound, so subtle it screamed for her attention, made her take a couple of bold steps toward the tree line encircling her home. She stared into the darkness, daring something to move while praying nothing would. Her heartbeat was keeping pace with the sounds of the tree frogs. Then it happened. A shadow of a man inched further into the woods. She dropped her bags and ran to seek the protection of her husband. Andy was one of the men called, and with flashlights, they combed the woods. Besides footsteps, nothing was there. Weeks would pass between incidents.

Sometimes the police were called. Too often, it was merely a feeling, a shift of leaves, a glimpse of something. There was never anything they could prove. The dark shadows continued to elude capture until the neighborhood would again go quiet. Sometimes, the calm would last long enough for the town to become comfortable again.

In the moments of quiet, a transformation was happening that would take the town years to discover. The disturbed lurker was changing into a monster. He was becoming more comfortable with his ability to elude the authorities. His imagination was growing each time he stood outside a window, daring himself to take the next step, imagining it enough times that it became inevitable.

MARY

Mary had become accustomed to being alone. The girls were now thirteen and eleven. Their weekends were becoming increasingly about friends, sleepovers, and even boys. Mary had tightened the reins every time the stories began again. No one argued, not the girls or Dan. They could be dropped off at the movies and picked up immediately afterward. They were only allowed to stay the night at close friends' houses.

Mary knew that darkness could be in someone she least expected, and she trusted very few people with her girls. She would visit with Sarah on those nights and even occasionally join them on their back porch and watch the stars light the sky. They never made Mary feel unwelcome, and she had to force herself to leave knowing inside it was not her place to be. She would drift back to her empty home, pour herself a small glass of wine, and pick up her latest novel. After a while, she even believed she was happy.

What amazed her was how fast the years could go by in that way. Junior high was a mere blip of time that led her to the dreaded years of high school. Not only did each school year mark the end of her time with her girls, but they also raised fears. What mistakes would her children make? In her quiet way, she prayed their fate would be so much better than her own. Would they know what a marriage should offer, or how a man should treat them?

Sadly, Mary wondered if she knew herself. How far she had fallen the night of her prom. Someone would have loved her. She wasn't meant to be sitting alone night after night. Now and then, she became so lonely that even the sound of Dan staggering up the steps was music in her quiet world.

She decided to give her marriage a chance. The thought of kissing Dan was so foreign that nervous bile rose in her throat. She wanted to pretend it was the excitement of what was nearly unknown that caused the sensation, a second first kiss. However, Mary knew she was faking desire.

What if he wouldn't even kiss her? Could she stand rejection from a man she felt was beneath her? She rose to peer out her window at the place Dan should be parked. The darkness sent a chill down her spine. The stories had started again, and even though the police were patrolling, she could not shake her fear. She couldn't be alone anymore. When Dan returned, she would begin again.

It was nearly two in the morning when she heard Dan's car pull in the driveway. She straightened her hair in her dresser mirror and went down the stairs to meet him. He threw his keys on the counter and sat at the kitchen table to untie his boots.

"I'm glad you're home."

Dan jumped at the sound of her voice. "Why? Did something happen?"

"No, I'm just happy to have company." She continued down the steps and sat in the chair next to him.

"Hmm. Are you now?" Mary took a deep breath. It would involve more effort than a few words to break through so many years of drifting.

"I've just felt a bit nervous here by myself with all these weird stories going around."

"I'm quite sure you're fine." He was trying to hurt her, but she refused to give up.

"I think I'm fine, too; however, it's nice to have you home." Silence filled the kitchen. "I was thinking maybe we could try to make some...some changes."

"Changes? What do you have in mind?"

"Well, maybe one day a weekend, we could plan something together."

Dan gave her a questioning look before standing, "We'll see." He headed up the stairs leaving Mary alone again.

That week Mary tried to have dinner on the table when Dan would be getting off work. Monday, he was two hours late. Mary had already cleaned up the kitchen and wrapped his meal when he returned home. They watched television in silence. Tuesday, he came home well after she was asleep. Wednesday, they ate their first meal together in years. It was only Shake and Bake chicken, but then Mary had never claimed to be a chef. She opened a bottle of Chardonnay, hoping it would make it more elegant. Each clank of the silverware stressed the awkwardness. At least, Mary told herself, there was an effort on both ends.

"You know, I was thinking we could get together with Sarah and Andy every now and then to play cards or something." Mary was desperate to rid herself of the strained silence.

"I guess." His words were huge to Mary since she knew that Dan lacked feelings for Sarah. He must care. Maybe there was hope for some level of companionship. She realized it might never be the level of relationship that Sarah and Andy experienced, but she needed something.

CHAPTER 13
1992
Sarah

T he paper hit the end of the driveway with a thud that echoed all the way into Sarah's living room. The sound demanded her attention in a way a person could change their tone to fit their mood. She was still wearing her housecoat, so she eased outside, looking each way before rushing to grab it.

Back inside, she poured herself a cup of coffee and settled in at the kitchen table. A nameless victim, but a crime they had all feared would find their sleepy town was the top story. She was raped in her home nights after complaining to the police that she felt she was being watched.

Sarah ran to the phone to call her friend.

Mary

There is no lonelier place a person can be than to be alone with a secret, or worse yet, a secret based only on suspicion, a feeling. What did she have to go by in reality? What proof was there except the darkness in his eyes and love so disguised it could

135

almost be abuse? How could Mary explain any of it to anyone? She had never even spoken to Sarah about the things that happened behind closed doors.

After Mary had decided to restart their relationship, she also had to start allowing him back into the bedroom. It was never something she wanted, but the stories became worse and worse, and she refused to let Dan slip away again. She couldn't be alone, especially after the first rape happened. Shortly after, a second rape occurred in their neighborhood. She would do anything not to be alone, even if it meant being intimate with Dan.

It took years for her to start to see a pattern. The friskier Dan was at home, the quieter the news. Then there were times it was quiet both places, but the rumors became louder. Kathleen would come in and out of the picture, and Mary suspected that when it became quiet in both her home and the town, Kathleen was fulfilling whatever sick hunger Dan was feeling. Kathleen probably thought she was coy getting away with her affair.

Her mother kept her informed sometimes. Mary was quite sure she didn't get the whole story and couldn't blame her mother for not being entirely forthcoming. After all, how does a mother tell her daughter such things? More people reported seeing Dan getting into Kathleen's car at lunchtime on and off through the years, and Mary knew that something had recently happened between them.

The last lunch ended with her squealing out of the parking lot and him yelling a few choice words in her direction.

What made her hate Dan most wasn't the affair, rather the fact that he would do it at her father's company with no care about the position it created for her parents. She knew that her father wouldn't fire him because that would hurt Mary financially. She was sure her father had many words with Dan. Mary hated how it must torment him to watch his son-in-law continually mistreat his daughter through the years.

Since the fight with Kathleen, Dan was angry all the time. He seemed stressed and often paced like an animal. She found him drinking straight from the bottle of whiskey they kept in their kitchen cupboard.

Since the children were grown and had moved out, Mary seldom commented about his habits. Cirrhosis of the liver could be an excellent friend to her, and if it had not been morally wrong, she might have prayed for it.

She looked at the phone for an answer. What could she say to the police? All she could say was that her husband was a bastard and he was acting very differently since the rapes began. Dan still had many friends, and she was quite sure some were the police officers that would have occasional beers at the pub Dan frequented. What would they say if she called? Would they only think she was crazy and tell Dan what she had done?

Or worse yet, what if they listened to her? What if she was right? It was one thing to suspect something and another to make it a reality. How could she live in this town? She would have to move from Sarah and Andy, people that had become family to her. What about her girls? Even though they were grown and out of the house, they were still nearby. How would they handle this? As much as Dan was a terrible husband, he was an okay father. The girls loved him despite his many flaws.

She thought of the many birthday parties she had planned through the years. Dan only occasionally showed up for them, and sometimes he only showed up once he was drunk. The girls may not have noticed, they were young, but Mary did.

As the girls got older, Dan was there to frighten off the suitors and make them feel protected. They accepted this as love. Mary had her doubts. Some people only cared about being bullies, and this is what Mary was sure he was thriving on instead. She hoped that the old saying that a girl marries someone that reminds them of their father would not hold true for Karen and Eva. There was so much better.

SARAH

Sarah busied herself in the kitchen for the once a month card game that had become a tradition for Mary, Dan, Andy, and herself. Sarah was hesitant when Mary first suggested it. In the end, she could not deny her friend. After the arrangement began to be a routine, the evening became almost bearable, like a sliver embedded under their skin. Andy could make polite talk with anybody, even if he didn't approve of them.

Kyle came into the kitchen, ready for a night out with friends. Sarah smiled at him as he tucked his t-shirt into his jeans. She didn't worry about his choices since Kyle had never given her cause for concern. He was his father's son, so easy to love.

He diverted her attention by placing a kiss on her forehead, so he could grab a ham biscuit she was preparing. She slapped his hand away and pretended to be annoyed. He let out a laugh while stuffing the large morsel in his mouth.

"So, where are you off to tonight?"

"The drive-in. John's driving, so I'm in good hands," Kyle said, reassuring her. "I won't have to worry about my car dying and stranding us."

"Well, come right home after. I don't like you out on the road at night." A horn honked in the driveway.

"No worries, Mom." He laid another peck on her cheek and wished her luck in cards. She watched until the door closed behind him. She was always amazed at the extent that she loved her children and how quickly her time with them went.

Amanda was a freshman at Virginia Tech and was hours away. She was still trying to get used to the house without her. Sometimes Sarah thought that she could smell her perfume as she passed by her bedroom at night. Her thoughts drifted to her daughter so often that she sometimes thought it would have been easier to have a limb amputated. Up to that point, it was the only loss she could compare it to.

Andy came out of the bedroom, freshly showered. "Need any help?"

"I've got it covered. You can get the cards ready, I guess."

Just then, they heard the knock on the door. Mary came in, full of energy and enthusiasm, followed by her dark shadow. Dan shook Andy's hand, and they quickly found the cold beers. The night always got better when the beer started to flow, and the tension eased. Sarah even found a quick moment in the kitchen to down half her beer before pasting the smile back on her lips.

After about an hour, Dan was up by quite a bit. One of the perks of having no conscience, Sarah thought, was the ability to lie very well. Dan's expression never changed. Maybe that was why Sarah was drawn to his face when one of them brought up the local news. It was like trying to see the bottom of a pond through a ripple. Whatever lay beneath the water was almost visible, but the level of distortion would remain unknown.

"Dan, did you hear another woman got raped right in her home?" Andy asked.

Sarah's eyes shot to Andy. He tried not to speak too much of the rapes except for the warnings he gave Sarah for her safety.

"I try not to watch the local news." Dan took a long puff of his cigarette. "They're just a bunch of amateur reporters. You can't really trust what they say, and most of what they report on isn't worth reporting anyway."

"That may be true most of the time, but you might want to start paying attention to it now. I don't even want to leave Sarah alone," said Andy.

Dan glanced at Sarah through a circle of smoke. "I wouldn't worry about her." Why did Sarah just feel like she was insulted?

Andy glared at Dan; his jab did not go unnoticed. "I'll tell you what, if anyone ever hurt my wife, I'd kill him before the police stood a chance to get near him."

Dan raised his eyes from his cards and looked at him. It seemed everyone was staring at Andy. "Well, Andy, look at you, sounding like mister

141

tough guy. I'm impressed." Andy took a large swallow of his beer, which Sarah was quite sure was only done to drown his words.

"I heard he takes something from his victims. The first woman had her watch taken and the second woman, a necklace," Mary said. It was an attempt to unlock the eyes of the men at the table, that had locked like antlers.

"It's a small town. It's only a matter of time before the police catch him," Sarah interjected.

The men were studying their cards, ignoring each other. Play went around the table another round in silence before Sarah began to think aloud. "Do you think it's the same person that was stealing the underclothes off of the lines years back and watching women through their windows."

"You know I wonder about that, too. You may have a point. He never was caught." Mary thought for a moment. "Some people are really sick. I hope they catch the bastard soon." Sarah couldn't know the many thoughts racing through Mary's mind.

Dan slammed down his cards, shaking the beer bottles and rendering silence. "Are we quite done with this ridiculous talk, or do I need to find someone else to drink a damn beer with tonight?"

"Let's relax, Dan. All right, ladies, on to better subjects," Andy said.

Andy gave Dan one last glance, and the game continued in quiet. Each swig lasted twice as long, as they all searched for the calm at the bottom of the bottle.

Mary lay in bed next to Dan. He was snoring as usual, since he did so every time he drank. The ceiling was white, with about four flaws spread across it. Mary figured they were nail-pops from the house settling through time. She wondered if the house was aware of being punctured as the nails found their way to the surface, or did it happen so slowly that it went undetected.

Mary knew each nail pop by heart. She stared at her ceiling nightly. In the beginning, it was while waiting anxiously for her new husband to come home to her and their baby. Over time, she realized he didn't care about coming back to them. He would stumble in the door, smelling of whiskey and perfume. His only thought would be of bed. She wondered how he could let those years fly by. Mary couldn't wait to be home with her baby. To touch her fingers and rub her cheeks. She would wake in the night just to peer into the crib and watch her babies sleep.

Years of rumors, neglect, hatred, children growing, and moving on had left her with what? A pretend marriage. She was sometimes surprised how little she cared what Dan was doing. The only thing that bothered her was when she bumped into people with their knowing glances. Some people carried pity, and some were empowered by their "secret." Having people act as if they had one up on her was the part that hurt the most. She wanted to scream sometimes, *I know, and I don't care!* Sarah, Andy, and all their children were her family. Dan was something she picked up on the way that she couldn't get rid of much like a venereal disease.

What if her fears were valid? What if the man next to her were a monster? There were moments when it was so evident that she became weak, and other times she felt like a drama-seeking teenager for thinking the father of her children could possibly be the man responsible for such evil.

Maybe these thoughts were why she still sat up at night, counting the nail pops. Instead, she told herself it was only a lousy marriage and forced herself back into reality. A reality that still lacked so much. She knew that Sarah had to have heard the rumors, too. She also knew that her friend was respecting her by not bringing them up. Sarah probably thought she stayed quiet about them herself because it was too painful. However, it was only painful because it didn't bother her at all.

Mary thought back to herself in high school. She knew, along with everyone else, that she was beautiful, and her confidence was hard to shake. Mary had an air of perfection without the edge of snobbishness. She had it all. She was never a girl to wait for a knight in shining armor to rush in to rescue her.

Mary had a vision, at one point, of the woman she would be and the man that would stand proudly beside her. He would be impressed by her intellect and style and want to show her off until her face gave way to time and her hands tired of work, and even then, he would love her. She stared at the nail pops and knew she could never impress the man next to her, and she didn't even care to try anymore. The smell of Old Spice covered with whiskey nauseated her.

Sometimes, as she stared into the night, she pictured her life as if she had met Andy first. Had she been the one to be at the diner that day, would he have noticed her? Most young men noticed her when she and Sarah were together. Then she would picture Sarah and Andy together, and she knew that he wouldn't have paid attention to her had she danced naked on the table next to Sarah. The idea of being envious of Sarah still startled her like hearing life-altering news every day of your life. She wondered how many more nails would slowly pierce through the ceiling in the years to come. She went to sleep dreaming dreams she would never share with a soul.

Mary generally worked the day shift at the hospital, but a colleague had begged her to cover her night shift. It was extremely tranquil for the first several hours, which bored Mary. She liked the hustle and bustle and thrived on the adrenaline rush of emergencies. She looked up at the clock and sighed, realizing she still had five hours to go. As she headed down the hall to check on an elderly man admitted for a heart attack, the familiar sounds of the doors sliding open and the gurney wheels heading down the hall caught her attention. Guilty pleasure filled her, and she told herself that if it weren't for people that thrived on this stuff, the world would be in trouble.

Two paramedics wheeled a woman Mary guessed to be in her thirties down the hallway. There was obvious trauma to her face, and Mary noticed that her tears were trickling down her blood-streaked cheeks. Mary guided the paramedics to the open room, and Dr. Ramsey was in the ER within moments.

"What do we have?"

"Thirty-two-year-old female. Attacked in her house. Her husband came home and found her trying to clean herself in the bathroom. He tried to get her to get in his car so he could drive her to the hospital, but she refused. He called the ambulance to encourage her to come in."

"I'm Dr. Ramsey. What's your name?" The woman continued to stare to the side.

"Her name is Claudine. I came home and found her bloody, and her clothes were ripped," a shaky voice responded from behind them.

The husband was standing by the door. He broke down crying, and something inside Mary froze.

"I think it was that bastard. I think he raped my wife."

Mary noticed the tears increase, and the woman's chin began to shake. The man reached the woman's bedside and grabbed his wife's hand.

"We'll get him, honey. I promise you we will get him, and he will pay for this." He buried his face in his wife's stomach and sobbed.

Dr. Ramsey motioned with his head for Mary to come with him.

"I'm going to clear the room and give you some privacy with her. She may be able to speak easier to another woman. Try to find out what happened. She may not be able to admit it in front of her husband right now." Mary could only nod like a robot.

"Sir, let's give your wife some privacy for a minute, and you can answer some questions for me in the hallway."

The man slowly let go of his wife's hand, and a procession of people left the room, leaving a painful silence. In all Mary's nursing experiences, she had never felt so uncomfortable and unsettled.

She walked to the woman's bedside, allowing her to stare away from the stranger beside her.

"I'm so sorry this happened." Why was she apologizing? "I want to help you. For me to do that, you need to answer a few questions. Can you do that?" The woman nodded, still staring toward the wall. "Did the man force you to have sex?" Mary heard a small sob, and the woman nodded slowly. "I'm so sorry. We're going to do all we can to help catch him." Mary held her hand and found herself looking at the floor in dismay.

She was shocked to hear the woman's voice. "I can still smell him." Mary's head shot up, and she found herself staring into her swollen eyes. "I can't stop smelling him. It's a smell I know, but I don't know the name of it. I can't stop smelling it." Then the woman lost herself to the tears that hid behind the dam. Mary held onto her, silently begging her not to remember the familiar smell of whiskey and Old Spice that had sickened her for so many years.

CHAPTER 14
1992
Sarah

Sarah shuffled down to the end of the driveway to pick up the morning paper. Mary's car was parked in front of her home, but Sarah remembered that she worked the night shift. She would be having her coffee alone while Mary slept in today. As she leaned down for the paper, the headline title jumped out at her, *Another Victim*. Was this four or five in only a few months? Something had turned the neighborhood pervert into a monster. She turned toward the house and was nearly run over by a young boy on his bike.

"Excuse me, Mrs. Turner."

"Morning, Tommy," Sarah called after the blur. She didn't know him well; despite the fact, this town was her family, and she suddenly felt protective of everyone in it.

She carried the paper to the kitchen table and poured herself a cup of coffee. Andy and Kyle were up early and off to work. The house was the kind of quiet that was treasured, not the type that lurked eerily around every corner. Her chair dragged across the tile, making an intrusive screech across the floor. The headline stared up at her.

Another woman of about her age was the latest victim. This time, the man took the woman's necklace, a cross on a gold chain. Was the bastard trying to mock God, or was he just truly lacking any conscience? In this quiet, peaceful town, women were now being told to lock their doors at night and not walk alone. It outraged her and petrified her at the same time.

She dropped the paper onto the table, raised her coffee cup to her lips, and sat back in her chair. From her kitchen table, she could easily see out her screen door to the cherry tree in full bloom. How could she shut out the sound of the birds, the smell of spring, the sun warming the ground ready to give birth to the patiently awaiting bulbs?

She set down her cup and walked to every window in her living room, spreading the window treatments as wide apart as she could. Then she opened the windows until the mingling breezes freshened the farthest corners of her home. She stood there, letting the curtains flap against her in the breeze, giving her a strength that she wasn't sure she really owned. With a deep breath, she turned away from the vulnerability the openness created and walked into her bedroom to shed her linen nightdress.

As she slipped it over her head, the distinctive sound of the screen door slamming to a close froze her in her place. She stood in only her undergarments, completely exposed. Her breath remained where she had last left it, deciding whether to be inhaled or exhaled. Somewhere in her brain, she heard the words, *Grab your clothes*, but her body never responded.

"Sarah?" Mary's voice cut through the ice that had frozen Sarah, and she exhaled.

"I'm changing. I'll be right there." She grabbed a pair of white capris and a pink top, still refusing to let in the darkness. She rushed to the kitchen, curious as to why Mary would be up so early after a night shift. Rounding the corner, she found herself facing Mary, who was disheveled and uncombed. She didn't know whether to laugh or be concerned that there was definite proof the world was amiss.

"You look like crap, girl. Why aren't you sleeping?"

"I wish I were, but I just can't. Do you have any fresh coffee?"

"Of course, I do."

The two women made their way to the kitchen. Sarah turned toward the counter to pour the warm comfort into Mary's cup while Mary found herself face to face with the reason for her insomnia.

"Were you reading today's paper?" Mary asked.

"Yes, can you believe this? I hope they catch this guy soon."

"Me too." Sarah sensed that something was weighing down Mary. "I was there when this woman came into the ER last night." Mary put her head in her hands and rested her elbows on the table.

"God, Mary. That must be troubling. It makes you feel a bit too close to it all, I'm sure."

"Yeah, I am definitely feeling too close to it all. She was so upset." Mary looked up at Sarah. "What's gonna happen when they catch him?"

"What do you mean? He'll go to jail where he deserves, and then everything will go back to normal."

Mary stared at the headlines if only to avoid her friend's eyes. "I wonder if it will be that easy."

"What do you mean? Well, I'm sure it won't feel normal to the victims for a very long time, but don't worry. I'm right across the street. We'll look out for each other," Sarah said. "They'll catch him soon, and this will all be a thing of the past. It won't be long before they have him behind bars, Mary."

"You know, I do think I need to get some sleep. Thanks for the coffee."

"Stop by when you wake up. You'll feel better after some sleep."

"I'm sure I will. I'll catch up to you later." Sarah watched Mary walking away until she gave a quick wave at the end of the driveway. She then shut the door and locked it behind her. Maybe she shouldn't push her luck.

All was quiet for another week, and then Sarah's Saturday began with yet another headline. This time a silver earring was taken from the victim. Sarah's hand, for some reason, reached to caress her own jewelry as if it somehow supported the victim and assured her of her safety at the same time.

Andy came out of the bedroom, was met with his coffee and a kiss. His eyes fell on the paper, and an image of a more anxious and angry man covered the Andy Sarah knew so well. "Seriously, Sarah, I want these doors locked at all times."

"Andy, nothing has happened to anyone during the day, and you are with me at night. You don't have to worry about me."

"Lock the doors, Sarah. It's not an option, or I'm going to hire someone to be at the garage more so I can be home."

"Andy, really."

"You heard me!"

Sarah was surprised by Andy's authoritative tone. "Okay." She wrapped her arms around his neck.

"Don't worry about me. I'll lock the doors, and I promise not to walk the streets at night."

"I just hope you're taking me seriously."

"I am." She put her arms around him while she placed a gentle kiss on his lips. Then she let her hand slide down the back of his head, holding him in place for just a moment to marvel at the love in his eyes before turning away.

"Don't forget Kyle has his game tonight."

"I would never forget such a thing. I'm supposed to help him practice his pitching today. I think he is just amusing his old man now. I don't have any more tricks to teach him."

"Maybe he just knows a good coach when he sees one." Sarah smiled at her husband, knowing that even though they were both showing a few new wrinkles that he had many good years left in him. "I'll be in my favorite chair watching."

Kyle came out of his bedroom; his hair was too short to be very messy. He headed directly to the fridge to drink from the orange juice container. "Kyle!" He replaced it after a few good swigs and kissed his mom on the forehead.

"Morning, Mom."

Sarah found herself caught in the middle of irritation and immeasurable pride. The very place Kyle knew where he could do no wrong. She rolled her eyes a bit before asking what he would like for breakfast. The storms that existed outside their home left them untouched for another day.

Andy came to the counter at the garage to get the keys for the next car. It had been a slow day, and he found the young assistant reading the paper at the counter.

"Any good news?"

"Not unless you consider the sixth victim good news."

Andy felt the acid rise in his throat. The muscles in his body tensed, and he felt sensations that he never felt before. It frightened him because he was a predictable person. Andy knew himself well and was always comfortable with who he was as a husband and a father. Despite this, recent events made him question everything. What was right? When he thought of anyone hurting Sarah, he felt a rage inside of himself that was so unfamiliar. He thought of Amanda walking around campus at night, and he felt defenseless. He knew he would do anything to keep them safe.

His earth seemed to be crumbling under his feet. No matter how hard he tried to hold on to his normal self, he felt something darker emerging. He rushed through the last oil change without thought. He could complete oil changes in his sleep after these many years.

"I'm going home for lunch today," Andy announced as he handed over the last set of keys.

"I'll hold down the fort."

"I know you will. Call me if an emergency comes in; otherwise, I'll be back in about an hour."

He was craving the normalcy and warmth of home. He could see Sarah through the screen door in her recliner with her television tray pulled up in front of her. He could hear Bob Barker calling down the next contestant, and he stood for a moment, watching Sarah taking a bite of her sandwich. He studied her, totally vulnerable yet defiant amid evil. Only a screen stood between her and the predator that haunted the streets. So many emotions flooded through him as he observed his wife that he could not tell what he was feeling at all.

An animal instinct alerted her to the fact that she was being watched, and she turned her attention to the screen door. When she saw Andy, she was quickly on her feet like a teenager caught in the act.

"What are you doing home? You didn't tell me you were coming home for lunch." She tried to find a pleasant everyday tone, but she knew she was in trouble.

"Why isn't the door locked?"

"I'm sorry, Andy. I can't explain it. It just makes me feel like he won if I have to lock my door on a lovely spring day."

"You listen to me, Sarah," Andy felt somehow possessed with an energy the monster had brought to their town. "They will catch this guy, and then you can sit with your door unlocked all you want. Until then, lock the damned door!"

Andy was overwhelmed with guilt when he saw the look of fear and confusion on Sarah's face; regardless, he had to be firm. He knew that if something happened to her, it would make him become something he couldn't control.

"I'm sorry. I really am. I promise you I'll keep the door locked until they catch him."

Andy stared at his wife for a moment and then walked the couple of steps it took to take her in his arms. "Sarah, I couldn't handle something happening to you. Just please be careful."

"I promise. I'm sorry." After the tension had eased, Sarah took out Andy's television tray and asked him to have a seat. She brought him in a glass of sweet tea and a BLT. Before long, they were both silently lost in the world of *The Price is Right,* where the mundane rhythm of the show gave their lives the consistency that they both needed.

SARAH

A package arrived, which seldom happened. Sarah excitedly picked it up from the front porch, turned back into her home, locked the door diligently, and started to search the package for clues of its origin.

She became even more excited when she saw the package was from Amanda. Carefully, she peeled away the wrapping and found a framed picture of Amanda along with a book and envelope. She pulled out the letter eager to be inside her daughter's world if only for a moment.

Dear Mom and Dad,

I thought you might enjoy seeing me in your living room in the evenings, so I'm sending you this picture. Wish I could be there more. Love and miss you much.

Amanda

P.S. Mom, I just finished reading this novel and thought you would like it. Let me know what you think.

Sarah could barely wait to sit back and read the book. Any connection to her daughter was so dear to her, and she cherished the thought of discussing it during their next phone call. Before she could get to the reading, though, she would need to hang her picture.

Opening the drawer that should have contained the hammer proved to be disappointing. It was one of the downfalls of having a handy husband; he was always leaving the tools behind wherever he last worked. Sarah didn't want to wait for Andy to come home. She sat at the counter, trying to think of where he may have left it and then remembered that Mary had tools in their shed. She knew Mary wouldn't mind if she borrowed anything of hers, but in this case, Sarah would have it returned before she got home from work regardless.

She unlocked the front door and headed across the street. There was an ominous silence resting over the neighborhood that felt foreboding. Everyone was on edge. Even the children were not allowed outside without an adult, which meant they were inside or at school. Sarah craved their energy and enthusiasm and could not wait for this all to pass.

There was a lock on the shed; however, Mary had told her where they hid the key sometime before. She lifted the rock half-hidden by a bush and found it in its case. Even though the lock was a bit rusted, Sarah was able to jimmy it open without much effort. She found a light switch that turned on the one working bulb. The toolbox lay on the workbench, and Sarah headed right for it. Unfortunately, it contained every standard tool except a hammer.

She placed her hands on her hips, and with a sigh, she scanned the dusty room. She noticed that under the bench was another toolbox. It apparently wasn't used often since several miscellaneous parts were laying on top of it. Keeping Amanda's smiling face in mind, she began to uncover the box and pulled it out for a better view. For a box that was so well hidden, it had little dust on it. Sarah thought this to be a good sign and opened it feeling quite sure she would soon be hanging Amanda's picture.

Nothing was in the upper compartment, and she began to doubt herself. Removing the top shelf of the toolbox, she found an old cloth. If she perceived this as strange, she did not allow herself to stop long enough for it to matter. As she lifted the fabric, she felt a light object fall onto her bent knees. She grabbed it quickly so she wouldn't lose it in the cracks of the shed floor. She caught the chain, and it swung from her fingers. What an odd object for a toolbox, she thought. Lifting the chain for a closer look, she noticed the quality and how clean it was for a piece of jewelry thrown in a toolbox. Then she saw the cross.

Neither Dan nor Mary was particularly religious. As her mind pondered why a cross would be in Dan's toolbox, an ugly realization began to push its way to the surface of Sarah's consciousness. She began to see the newspaper articles in front of her, and she scanned them again in her memory. She felt as if she were suffocating behind her racing heartbeat. In a crazy frenzy, Sarah dug through the toolbox for more answers; a silver earring, a pair of underwear, a lock of hair cried out to her. She stumbled backward, away from the box, as if it could reach out and drag her in with everything else.

As soon as she could move, she scrambled across the floor and tried to put everything back in place just the way she found it. She couldn't get across the road fast enough, and this time she locked the door behind her without a second thought.

CHAPTER 15

1 9 9 2
S a r a h

The rest of Sarah's day was a blur, passing in a haze of crying and wringing her hands. She could handle this. She had to be able to handle this. Every idea spun in her mind: call Andy, call Mary, call the police. Each envisioned plan ended the same way. Mary would be destroyed. In the end, she decided she would handle it on her own. Sarah would quickly realize she had made the second wrong decision of her life.

Sarah stood in the local pub with tears pooling in her eyes. She couldn't tell whether they were from staring so intently or from the smoke that overpowered the room. She was accustomed to cigarette smoke but had never been in a barroom filled with thirty men smoking all at once. Every time the door swung open, another story entered the room. There were the young romances, the men's night out, the loner looking for a fix. Sarah only cared about the one story, the story she wanted to end.

After she had finished two drinks, Dan burst through the door as if he was a local celebrity, and by his side was Kathleen. She looked so broken that Sarah had a hard time hating her. Her sins had caught up to her. Dan only showed a slight surprise to see Sarah through the haze. He whispered something in Kathleen's ear, and dutifully she went and sat in a booth seat. His eyes fell once again on Sarah, and he began heading toward her.

Sarah lifted her chin to show her confidence, but inside, her head spun as she embraced what she was about to do. Tonight, she would be the predator and not the prey, but she questioned how intimidated a grizzly bear could be when confronted by a meager rabbit. She swallowed the last bit of whiskey and took a deep breath.

"Well, look who decided to go slumming tonight," Dan said with a sickening smirk.

"I have some things to discuss with you, and I figured I'd find you here."

"Did Mary send you here to check on me?"

"Mary doesn't know I'm here, and she would never ask me to come to this place."

"Well, then, what makes you think what I do is your business? If Mary has a problem with who I hang out with, she can tell me."

"I don't care about who you hang out with."

"And I don't care why you came down here." With that, Dan turned to walk away. Before he could take a full step, Sarah called out.

"I was in your shed!"

163

Dan turned back so quickly, putting his face within inches from hers. "What are you trying to say, Sarah?"

"I know it's you. I found everything." Even though Sarah should have felt powerful with her information as she stared back into Dan's dark, empty eyes, she felt nothing except terror as if she was staring into the pits of hell.

"You need to be very careful with what you are saying right now, Sarah. I would think very carefully before you continue talking."

Sarah's mouth felt like liquid metal was oozing down her throat. She swallowed hard but could not rid herself of the taste. "I'm giving you one chance. You are to leave town. Pretend you're leaving Mary and never look back. Stay away from the girls and the town. If you are gone in two days, I keep my mouth shut. After that, if you're still here, then I go to the police."

A long moment passed as Dan stared into Sarah's eyes. His heavy breathing left the air toxic. His fumes lingered between them until finally, he spoke.

"You are on dangerous ground, Sarah." Whiskey filled spit hit her cheeks. "You are on very dangerous ground."

CHAPTER 16

Decision Three

1992

Amanda

Amanda couldn't wait to get home. All the way there, she pictured the comforts that she had missed while away. Sometimes Amanda felt that because everything was so tranquil and pleasant in her home, she could go anywhere just knowing it would be there when she returned. The security she had always felt was a springboard to her future.

She pulled into the driveway and allowed herself a moment to look at the house as an outsider. It was a well-kept home, but never fancy. Azaleas bloomed a couple of times a year to give the appearance that a gardener lived inside. However, when their time passed, the yard diminished to only a somewhat manicured patch of different greens. Her mother's place was inside, and her father was not a fancy man. The house was a mirror of their personalities, and she loved the simplicity of it.

She swung open the door and announced, "I'm home!" She had expected the usual excitement. Instead, something felt flat. An energy that did not belong encircled her family, and she was yet to know its source.

"Hey, Amanda. Mom thought you'd like to go out to eat, so there is no home cooking for you tonight," Kyle said, while offering a quick hug.

"I'm good with that."

Sarah came over and quickly embraced her daughter. "It's good to have you home, Amanda." Sarah drifted immediately back to the kitchen, where she put away dishes.

"Where's Dad?"

"He's putting on his final touches, so don't bother sitting down. I'm starved!" Kyle grabbed his jacket and stood by the door.

"When are you not starved?" She swatted the top of his head, messing his thick brown hair.

"You're just jealous because I have you by six inches."

"Five and a half at best." They both glanced in the kitchen as a plastic bowl bounced across the floor with an unwelcome clang. Sarah shuffled quickly to grab it and mumbled words neither Amanda nor Kyle could decipher.

"Is something wrong? It seems like... I don't know, just weird, I guess."

"Mom's been nervous all day. I thought it was because she was worried the house wouldn't be clean enough for you to come home to, but maybe not."

"Let me go talk to her." Amanda walked up behind her mother without being noticed. "Can I help you, Mom?"

Sarah jumped at the sound of her voice. "Oh, no, I'm so sorry, Amanda. I'm just distracted today."

"Why? Is something going on? Is everything okay with Dad?" Amanda couldn't even imagine what would shake her mother's world if it weren't something to do with one of them.

"No, I'm fine. Everything is fine."

Andy came out of the bedroom, showered and groomed.

"Amanda! My girl is home."

"Hi, Daddy." Her father's hug felt familiar and less strained than the atmosphere surrounding it.

Dinner involved a lighthearted conversation between the three of them. They had all given up asking what was bothering Sarah but could not stop themselves from looking at her throughout the meal to catch her distant gaze.

That night, Amanda lay in her bed, listening to the quiet of their home. An occasional creak would break the silence as the house stretched before its rest. She thought of the countless nights her mother would sit on the edge of the bed combing out her long brown hair. Amanda loved to wear linen nightgowns that were outdated, according to some people, but felt comforting to her. Sarah would tell her stories of the nights she had spent in her very room as a young girl. Silly sleepover stories about her and Mary that made Amanda feel as if she almost shared in the memory.

By Amanda's request, the very picture of Sarah's mother sat on her nightstand, and Amanda found herself, as a young girl, kissing her unknown grandmother goodnight just as her mother had done. She always knew the stories were coming to an end when Sarah began to braid her hair. She loved to sleep in a braid so her hair would look naturally wavy in the morning.

Amanda thought of all those memories trying desperately to chase away the feeling that was building inside of her. Something was wrong.

SARAH

Sarah knew she hadn't thought through her plan after she left the bar that night. Her nerves had begun to pulse, reaching every part of her body. Trying to make breakfast for Andy and Kyle was impossible. She dropped the eggs while getting them out of the fridge, burnt the toast, and splashed coffee all over the table while she tried to refresh Andy's cup.

"What's up with you, Sarah? You seem so jittery. Not to mention you tossed and turned all night."

"Nothing, I just have a bunch on my mind. Amanda is coming home, and I need to shop and clean and... I don't know. I'm just thinking of a million things."

She couldn't tell him that she just realized that there was no proof of the items in the shed. She should have taken a picture of them or something before going to Dan. She was sure that he would move them the first chance he got.

"Amanda's not going to care if the house is clean, and I was thinking we should go out to dinner anyway. It might be nice since she doesn't get home often. You know, give her a chance to visit the old stomping grounds."

"Or maybe she'll like a nice home-cooked meal."

"Whatever you choose, honey, but stop stressing over it."

"You're right." Sarah took a deep breath before she could create any more suspicion. However, her mind kept racing with a million questions. How would she know if he left? Would he disappear? Would Mary come to her, crying and upset? Was she ready to be responsible for those feelings? What about the place he moved to next? She was protecting her friend and her town, but another unsuspecting and underserving woman would be the next victim because she wasn't calling the police. Whatever happened to them would be her fault, too.

"Sarah, I said I'm gonna get going."

"Oh, I'm sorry, Andy. I just..."

"I know, I know, you have a lot on your mind." He gave her a quick kiss and was out the door.

Sarah busied herself all day cleaning, making a shopping list, and trying to read the book Amanda had sent to her. She loved that her daughter discussed novels with her. Every story ended with their private book club. But no matter how many times she tried to read a paragraph, she could not absorb a thing. She found herself drifting off to sleep with the book in her lap.

Dreams circled in her head, dark visions, but she couldn't place what frightened her about them. They were only a series of images, a stranger's face, a dark road, and then a feeling of someone watching her. She watched herself running down a dark street. Her home loomed in the distance, but no matter how hard she ran, the house would not get closer. In her dream, Andy came out onto the front porch, and the screen door slammed shut behind him. The sound jolted her out of her sleep as she realized that the screen door slammed shut in her reality as well. Andy stood above her, watching her sleep. The end of day one was closing in on her, and there was still no word from across the street.

Friday morning began the start of day two, two endless days of waiting Dan out. Amanda would be home soon. She had decided to scrap her shopping list and go with Andy's idea. They would go to the local diner that Amanda had always loved. Nothing fancy, they would have burgers, fries, and an assortment of milkshake flavors; tastes so familiar and comforting. Sarah decided it would make everything feel normal for just a moment, at least. She was wrong. Amanda burst into the room like a ray of sunshine, but even her daughter could not chase away the darkness.

Sarah couldn't stop thinking that there were only a limited number of hours before day two was complete. What had she done? She now had to be true to her word, and it frightened her more than anything she had ever experienced.

The burger lay almost untouched at dinner as she found herself continuously looking at her watch. It was as if being connected to the time would somehow make things happen. Sarah's mind swam around so many thoughts, keeping her dangerously close to drowning in what-ifs.

The chatter in the car on the ride home encircled her but could not penetrate her thoughts. She glanced at Mary's house as they approached. Only one light was on, the one in the bedroom. She desperately wanted to know if Mary was alone. Was she celebrating or crying? Either way, day two was over.

Sarah woke early and showered. She was determined to enjoy her daughter before she headed back to school the next day. Sarah made a promise to herself to be a better actress, at least, for the weekend. She went into the kitchen with her chin held stubbornly high as she prepared the coffee.

"I was hoping you would have some coffee waiting for me." Mary had managed to get almost in the kitchen before Sarah even knew she was in the house. She studied Mary's face to see if she would be breaking the big news to her, but there was only the smile that Sarah had grown accustomed to through the years.

"Perfect timing. It just finished brewing." Sarah's words came out evenly, but her hand shook as she poured the hot liquid. "You haven't joined

172

me for coffee in weeks, it seems." She stared at the cup as she handed it over, not daring to look at her friend. Why did she feel so guilty? She was doing this to help her.

"Believe it or not, I've been sleeping in lately. Maybe I'm getting old." Or, she thought, she was becoming too afraid of her husband to sleep next to him and found herself exhausted every morning.

"Really? I knew you would eventually catch up to me. Well, don't get too old too fast. I look forward to our morning chats." She handed Mary her cup. "So, how is everything?"

"Oh, about the same. I go to work, I come home, eat dinner by myself, and wait for Dan to come home." "You can come over and join us for dinner whenever you want."

"Thank you, but I've actually started liking my quiet time after work. I would be an awesome single person." Something inside Sarah smiled like she was given the go-ahead from up above.

"You have always been strong enough for anything, Mary. I'm quite sure you would be a great single lady. That's until word got out that you're on the market. Then you'd be snatched up so quickly you wouldn't have time to get lonely."

"No, thank you. I think I would steal my friend away from her husband, go on a few great girl trips, rediscover our youth, and then return you in almost one piece."

"That sounds very tempting," Sarah said.

They both sipped their coffee, silently envisioning their future escapades. Escape was sounding quite appealing to Sarah.

Amanda came into the kitchen wearing sweatpants, a big t-shirt, and tousled hair. She stretched her arms in the air and yawned dramatically. Always beautiful, Sarah thought to herself. Andy may not have thought Amanda would notice if the house was clean or not, but Sarah knew as she came in and took a deep breath that Amanda was breathing in her home. It was a home full of charm and warmth; it was her gift to them.

Mary immediately stood to hug her. It was soothing watching the closeness between her daughter and best friend.

"Look at you, Miss Sunshine. Have you developed your love of coffee yet?"

"It's more of a need."

Amanda filled them both in on her classes and late-night studying as she hugged her mug in her hands. After a couple of cups, Mary announced it was time for her to run. Sarah watched as she waved on the way out the door. Nothing was different. Nothing happened. It was up to her again, but that would have to wait until Monday when life returned to normal.

CHAPTER 17
1 9 9 2
S a r a h

Monday was a day Sarah would remember vividly for the rest of her existence. The air was fresh, the kind of sunny day where she wanted to wash the sheets just to put them on the line to dry, to soak up the day so she could wrap herself up in it at night. She wanted to get lost in the fresh, crisp world of new beginnings, but beginnings with promise, not fear.

The newspaper sat at the end of the driveway, holding within it the events of the night. Sarah wondered as she unlocked the door if it were even possible that Dan would have struck again. For a moment, she felt pride in the fact that she may have saved someone she knew from the agony of his disease. As she began to open the door, the phone rang, and she stopped to answer it.

"Morning, Mom."

"Morning, Amanda. Is everything all right?"

Amanda generally wouldn't call so soon after leaving. "Everything is good with me. I was just calling to check on you. You seemed so distracted this weekend."

"I'm sorry, Amanda. Everything's fine. Honest. I just have a lot on my mind; that's all."

"That's what you kept saying, but I feel like there is something. Would you like to talk about it?"

"Not really. I feel better already," Sarah lied. Amanda paused long enough to see if her mother would change her mind and talk.

"Well, then, I guess I'll let you go. I love you, Mom."

"I love you too, Amanda."

Sarah decided to open the kitchen windows before grabbing the paper. As she lifted the final window, she heard the front door shut. The sound surprised her since Andy had left for the garage hours before, Kyle was at school, and she knew Mary was working. As she turned toward the living room, she saw Dan stagger a bit by the couch. Any hint of fear froze in time as she tried to make sense of his image standing before her. Her skin prickled at the sight of him, and even ten feet from him, she could smell whiskey. He must have been drinking all night.

"Is Andy around?" The words slurred out of his mouth, and it made her stomach sour to be near him.

"Dan, why are you here? I don't have anything else to say to you."

"You have that right! You have no business trying to threaten me, bitch," Sarah stiffened. She had never had someone call her a bitch before, and it crossed a barrier into an unfamiliar and dark world.

"Dan, you need to leave..."

Dan took three giant steps lurching toward her, and she found herself cowering from his massive frame.

"Don't you ever tell me what to do again, bitch! Check the shed, Sarah. I think you were very mistaken. You should have kept your damn mouth shut!"

Why hadn't she moved them? Why hadn't the simple idea that he might move the items ever cross her naive mind? She was realizing too late how way out of her league she was.

As the last word left his lips, Dan's hands hit her chest, throwing her against the wall. She cried out as her head hit the hard surface, and she felt the lump already taking form.

"What are you thinking? Get the hell out of my house." She put her hands down on the floor to try to push her way up. As she did, Dan's hands grabbed the back of her hair, pulling her across the floor to the back part of the kitchen.

Her mouth was screaming stop, but it was falling on the ears of an animal. The one motion set Dan on a path that no words could stop. She felt Dan grabbing at her underclothes under her dress as she kicked to free herself. His hand went over her mouth once again, hurling her head into the ground. Her teeth closed on his palm, hoping to release his grip only to find her face slapped with the back of his hand. The action determined Sarah's destiny, and she whimpered to herself, closing her eyes to the world.

She lay with her face toward the cupboard, and as she slowly opened an eye, she saw his face in her side vision. So close, she could see each pore that breathed out the fumes of whiskey. She began looking at her hands and the long, sharp nails that started to take the shape of knives. All she had to do was pierce his skin and slice with all her strength down his face. It could not save her, but it would mark him as her attacker. Everyone would be able to put their injuries together, and there would be no denying who had done these evil things. Her mind willed her hand to move, but she knew in doing so she would also be scarring her beloved friend. There would be another way, and she would find it. It would be a way that he alone would pay.

If she could have stopped the world from knowing, of bringing this pain to Andy, she would have done it, but he would know the minute he saw her. She sat on the floor, beaten and sore. Dan's final words repeating in her head until she would have done anything to silence her brain.

"Tell Andy, Sarah, and kiss your perfect world goodbye." He rocked back in forth in his drunken stupor while he zipped his jeans. "You heard him,

Sarah, he would kill me." He smirked to himself. "Or he would try. Then what Sarah? Kiss your precious husband goodbye. If he comes after me, he will either be in prison or dead. I think you'll learn to keep your mouth shut now."

As soon as she heard the door shut behind him, the tears began to flow. She crawled to the shower. She knew she would need to call Andy, but she would be clean of Dan when he arrived. She scrubbed herself until her skin was raspberry red and sat under the hot flowing water, trying to wash the memory away. She would learn, though, that it would never go away.

The phone rang in the garage, and Sarah went on autopilot. She would never completely remember what she said to Andy, but before she knew it, the house was full of police. Andy would be sitting by her side one moment and then circling in some frantic mode, not knowing what to do. Sarah felt drugged. She couldn't focus on her words, but she knew enough to describe the attacker as a male wearing a ski mask, and no, she couldn't tell them anything that would help them identify him.

MARY

Mary went through the motions at work. She heard the report come in that there was yet another

179

victim. This woman refused to go to the hospital. The nurses gossiped about it as they came in and out of the patients' rooms. Mary stayed silent and just shook her head in dismay the way she thought she should. She was finishing up her shift, and the fresh nurses were coming in to take over. Mary wrote her final notes into the last patient's charts. Routine information she found herself reciting in her sleep. Meghan, a young new nurse that seemed to have all the gossip, was taking over for Mary.

"Meghan, Mr. Phillips is quite ornery today, so be on your toes. The doctor upped his pain medication, so maybe it'll help calm him down." Meghan looked at Mary with a peculiar expression and did not respond.

"Did you hear me, Meghan?"

"Yes, sorry, Mary. It's just, well, I don't know how to tell you this, but I think you know the latest victim." Mary's brain scanned everyone she could think of, somehow not even glancing Sarah's way.

"I do? Who was it?"

Meghan stared a moment before saying, "It was your neighbor, Sarah."

Sheer panic raced through her body, and she heard herself saying, "Oh, my God. Oh, my God," as she ran for the exit. She couldn't remember the drive home. Her hands held tight to the steering wheel, and she pulled herself so close she could feel it when she breathed as if in some way it would get her to Sarah faster. She pulled into her driveway, well-aware of the last police car idling there. As she jumped out of her car, ready to sprint to her friend, she saw Andy walking out of the house side by side with the officer. He noticed Mary and, with just the lift of his hand, let her know they needed space.

Of course, they did, but why did she feel so much like she was the criminal? How could he have done this to Sarah? She stood motionless, not knowing which way to go. Either Dan was more malicious than she could have ever imagined, or maybe she was wrong. Maybe this meant that it wasn't Dan. He would know he couldn't get away with it. Sarah's rape had to prove she wasn't married to the rapist. This horrific tragedy might just be what she needed to relieve herself of all the guilt she had been feeling. The wind blew through her hair, whispering the truth, the truth she wanted terribly to deny.

CHAPTER 18

1 9 9 2
S a r a h

As the days passed, they both knew Andy had to return to work and leave Sarah alone in the house. Sarah could see the stress getting to him physically. He was unable to eat, and he once mentioned his heart felt like it was in a constant race. Andy drank his coffee slowly the morning that he was to return and stretched out his morning routine as long as he possibly could. When it was time, he took Sarah in his arms. After a long embrace, he turned toward the door that had a new deadbolt shining on it like a knight in shining armor. It was the best one Andy could find. Sarah knew this because Kyle said they looked at several stores before selecting one.

Sarah would not be opening the windows, no matter how many cardinals begged her to hear their song. She followed Andy to the door and leaned against it for several minutes after he left. She was alone. Amanda begged to come home, but Sarah could not stand the thought of seeing her, of seeing the look in her eyes as she saw her mother as a victim for the first time. Instead, she paced unproductively pleading for the clock to bring lunchtime, Andy, and *The Price is Right*. She needed the comforts of routines, but with Andy by her side.

The clock ticked slowly, and she began to understand why animals flee their cages despite the fact they kept the dangers out, that tingling feeling alerting them to the dangers around them and the suffocating feeling of being trapped and vulnerable. She had nowhere to go. Nowhere felt safe. The quiet of the house strained her ears. Painfully, she listened for each crack of the worn, hardwood floor, each turn of their tarnished metal doorknob.

She went again and checked the lock, peered through the front window at the empty street. A squirrel scampered across the lawn, always leery of the neighborhood dogs that sought to toy with the weaker species. She let the drapes fall between herself and the world. The sheer white material was beginning to yellow; a fly laid dead on the window sill. She turned and left it for some other day.

Eleven thirty, Andy would come home anytime, and she would be able to breathe. Sarah went to the freezer for a dinner that should have been planned yesterday. Frozen chicken and a tenderloin she couldn't remember buying stared back at her. Whatever she had once planned for these lifeless creatures was unknown to her. No spice could bring these meals to life. Sarah shut the freezer door and saw the greasy fingerprints dotting the handle. The Windex remained untouched under the kitchen cabinet, the bottle too heavy to lift. She could only lay her head upon the cool door as if it was an old friend consoling her.

The phone's ring startled her. She found herself staring at it as if Dan's words were seeping through the cords. She heard him. She felt him once again holding her down, his words thick in her ear. "Tell Andy, Sarah, and kiss your perfect world goodbye. He will either be in prison or dead."

The phone rang again, and she walked toward it, watching it's every vibration. Again, it rang, and her hand reached for it. "Hello."

"Sarah, are you okay? What took so long to answer?" She hated hearing the pain in Andy's voice.

"I was..." her eyes searched the room finding her scrub bucket deserted in the corner, "I was cleaning the bathroom. Sorry, I didn't hear the phone over the water."

"Sarah, I'm sorry I can't come home for lunch today. I have an emergency repair. I'm sorry. Are you going to be all right?"

"Of course," her eyes locked on the deadbolt of the front door double checking it with her mind. "Andy, you don't have to worry about me."

"I love you, Sarah." In the quiet moment before he spoke again, she pictured him with his head cradled in his hand, rubbing away the sadness. His voice came quietly. "I'll be home early, okay."

"I'm okay. Don't worry."

"I don't think I'll ever be able to stop worrying."

Hatred rose in Sarah's throat like acid. Andy could never know it was Dan. She knew Dan was right. Andy would get revenge; he would kill him, and then she would lose him. He could never know.

"I'll see you tonight. I love you, too."

Sarah hung up and listened to the steady beating of her heart. How long could it beat so hard? The clock ticked. Her chest tightened. She couldn't be brave any longer. She raced across the kitchen, a prisoner with an opening. She grabbed the bread and ham, slapped on a slice of Swiss cheese, and splattered mustard across her counter. Then she grabbed two coca-colas and a bag of Fritos, threw them in a bag and headed toward the door, then came to a dead stop. She could do it. She told herself again. She could do it. She looked across the street. The beat-up, blue Ford was nowhere to be seen. She rushed to her Pinto, shined and well-kept by her husband. The keys rattled in her hands, seeking the ignition. The engine started, and her heart began to calm.

Andy's shop was only a couple of miles away, but she seldom went there. The bells jingled, alerting the young man at the desk of her arrival. His name was printed on the front of his blue coveralls, Matt.

"Hello, can I help you, ma'am?"

"I'm Mrs. Turner. I came to have lunch with Andy."

"Oh....Oh. Let me get him." She saw the thoughts go across his face. How would he know? Did Andy... No, he wouldn't have told him, but surely, he watched the news. Surely, he knew why his boss had taken so many days off. Would she ever feel like she wasn't wearing this disgrace?

Andy came in through the doors leading to the garage. His arms were around her immediately. Sarah buried her face in his coveralls and breathed in his warm scent. Her mind raced, trying to find a way she fit in there, why she could stay forever.

"What are you doing here?"

"I decided to surprise you with lunch since you couldn't come home," she smiled up at him as if he couldn't read her thoughts. His warm, blue eyes met her gaze, searching her as if looking away could cause her to disappear.

"Ham and Swiss, your favorite."

"Do you mind sitting with me while I work?" Sarah looked behind her and saw the family waiting for their car. The father glanced down at his watch, apparently estimating how much time their little conversation had set him back. The mother was trying to entertain an antsy little boy with chocolate milk stains down the front of him. Her high-pitched mommy voice did not match the stress between her brows.

"Sure, I've never watched you work before."

The car was lifted off the ground with the front tire removed. Sarah settled herself on Andy's toolbox and got out the sandwiches before she noticed the grease covering Andy's hands.

"I think I might have to be the assistant." She held out the sandwich so that Andy could take a bite, and then pulled a piece of ham off for herself. As usual, lately, the food weighed on her tongue. She had to force herself to swallow.

"So, what happened to their car?"

"They hit something in the road and broke the brake line. Luckily, the husband pulled over to check for damage, or they would've been in real danger."

"A brake line breaks that easy?"

"Not really easy. It was an unlucky hit. The tube is metal, so whatever it was must have hit it pretty hard. It just put a small hole in it, so they didn't lose their brakes right away."

Sarah held out the sandwich again but could not take another bite herself.

"Can I see it?"

"Sure, my little assistant. Come on down here." She lay down next to him and wondered for a moment why she had never done this before. His grease-covered hand reached up and touched the thin tube, so vital to the car's survival. Her hand followed his, brushing against it.

"It's pretty hard. I'm surprised it broke."

"Yes, it is. Could you hand me my tube cutter?"

"Tube cutter?"

"It's the thick silver and black one."

Sarah picked it up, studying it, remembering it. She watched how Andy twisted it around the tube and how the last bit of brake fluid dripped slowly hitting the floor with finality.

"What would have happened if he didn't notice the break?"

"Every time he tapped the brakes, it would have pumped out more brake fluid." He stopped to focus on the job, letting out a small grunt as the broken part of the tube was freed. "What's worse was it was a front tire. Those are the most important brakes for stopping."

She glanced through the window at the family; the boy was shaking the gumball machine; the father was pacing. Such a simple thing, a little tube, and this family could have had such a different fate. If they were meant to die, they wouldn't have found the broken brake line. It didn't seal their fate when the brake line broke. It wasn't their time, so fate intervened.

Sarah stared at the boy with his hand stuck up into the machine, the mother's hair now dangling out of her clip. They survived this because they were meant to. Her mind began twisting around the idea until it made complete sense. She wouldn't actually be responsible. If it weren't meant to happen, fate would intervene.

"Assistant, did you forget me?" She looked away from the family. It was her answer. Sarah smiled down at Andy. His scruffy face, the same one that she had looked up to for over twenty years. The gray hairs had started to show in the day's stubble. She knew what she needed to do.

CHAPTER 19
1 9 9 2
M a r y

Mary called the house each day, but Andy politely let her know that they needed time. Friday night, he called to say Sarah was ready to see her the following day. Mary paced her kitchen, for the first time, not knowing what she could possibly say to her life-long friend. Then it hit her. Mary ran to get her recipe box and searched for one of Sarah's favorites. She would speak through food.

Saturday morning, Mary woke up early to cook the lasagna and prepare a salad for Sarah's family. She scanned the directions and meticulously followed them. Mary had watched Sarah make lasagna a million times and secretly envied her abilities to provide warmth and comfort through food. She could do this. She lay each noodle down carefully, hoping that she could harness even the smallest bit of Mary's power with her inept abilities. However, as she placed the meal in the oven, she knew better. Nothing could heal Sarah's wounds.

While the lasagna cooked, she chopped the vegetables for the salad. She stopped at the idea of homemade dressing and added the store-bought ranch to her basket of food instead. As she was about to walk out the door, Dan came out of the bedroom, showered and dressed like he was going somewhere.

"I'll help you carry that over."

Mary looked at the stranger before her. Again, the same struggle to understand overwhelmed her. Was he acting helpful because he genuinely felt bad for their family? That would mean it wasn't him. If that wasn't the reality, then why, why would Dan want to carry the food over to them? Nothing made sense.

Andy and Kyle were out by Dan's truck. Mary's face struggled to find the right expression. Her smile was so out of place, but the appropriate expression was too foreign. Kyle and Andy stopped their quiet discussion as they saw Mary and Dan approaching. They seemed to be struggling with these new emotions as well.

When she reached Andy, she stretched out her arms to offer her portion of the meal. Her mouth began to utter something; however, she was not aware of what it would be. Before the words could surface, she started crying. Kyle took the salad, and Andy took her in his arms and let her cry into his shirt. From her angle, she could see Sarah's silhouette through the screen, slipping back into the darkness of the house.

Was she coming out? What made her turn away? "Can I go in and see her?"

Andy glanced at the house. "She said she's ready." Mary began walking toward the front door. It felt as if there had been a death and, in many ways, there had been. She knew she might never see her friend as she used to be again.

SARAH

From inside the house, Sarah watched Mary heading toward her, but quickly turned her attention back to the men. She couldn't hear their words, but by the way Dan patted her husband and son on their shoulders, she was sure he was offering his condolences. Pure hatred spread through her. She would find the courage to destroy him, and she would not wait long.

"Sarah?" The shaky voice of Mary drifted through their house. It was time to face the world, and it would begin with her friend. The friends held each other with quiet sobs muffled into each other's shoulders.

"I'm so sorry, Sarah. I..."

"Don't. Please don't try to find the right words because there aren't any. I will be okay. Eventually, I will be okay." Sarah could not make eye contact with Mary because she knew that no matter how hard she tried, the only way for her to be okay was to change Mary's world forever.

It wasn't the next day or the day after that when she chose to do it. She let the thoughts swirl in her mind forming a plan, watching when Dan left for work and when he came home. There was no pattern to his return, but it wouldn't matter. She would need to do it in the middle of the night.

Andy never brought his toolbox in, so she scrambled to find moments when he showered or fell asleep when she could check to see if the tube cutter was always there. She touched the silver handle, felt the sharpness under her finger. Andy was showering, so for the fourth time, she raced to find her weapon. It had begun to feel natural in her hand. Sarah's faded flowered apron became her accomplice, and she slid it in the pocket that used to hold butterscotch candies she would sneak throughout the day. How many times did the kids hear the wrappers and come racing in for theirs?

Bringing it in the house made it real, the decision final. Sarah heard the water cut off in the shower, and she raced around the kitchen, trying to find a place that Andy would not look. Sarah settled for the far back of the utensil drawer. The bathroom door opened as she whirled around, backing up to the drawer as if it could scream out her secret. Andy smiled at her suspiciously and then walked into the bedroom. The water boiled behind her splattering on her arm, a pain she accepted.

Dinner was polite but quiet; both still feeling the pain. Each of their mental distractions disguised her nervousness. She never slept once they climbed into bed. She watched the clock tick through the hours.

Andy began his quiet snore around ten. She heard Kyle come home from the football game, and she went out to hug him and check in with him. He was staying so busy lately. She heard Dan's truck pull in his driveway around midnight. She could picture him stumbling over the pebbled walkway and could hear the clanking of keys as they fell on the cement stoop followed by his mumbled voice through the still air. Then, all she heard were the tree frogs and crickets, which would soon be her only witnesses. The clock chimed, and she saw three o'clock. It was time. She turned in her bed and watched Andy breathe for a moment. His face was at peace in his sleeping state. She tried to memorize it while she allowed them both a moment to say goodbye to a part of her that was too tarnished to keep.

The house was quiet. So quiet it felt like a different world, or maybe she was just a different person in the same world. She crept out of bed and went to the kitchen. Her hands slightly shook as she reached for the tube cutter she had hidden earlier. It had waited like a solitary soldier for its mission to arise. Sarah stood in her nightgown, bare feet sticking out, and tried to find balance on her cold kitchen floor, a floor that seemed to spin around her. She placed her hands, still gripping the cutter, upon her counter and breathed in deeply. *Please, if I shouldn't do this, let someone wake up.* The house responded with silence. It would not help her with her decision.

With another deep breath, she turned so that she could see the front door through her living room. Sarah knew that once she crossed it, she would be going somewhere that she could not easily return from, but she had thought it out. If she didn't do this Sarah would see Dan every day; she would sit through card games with him in the very kitchen he raped her; she would know that across the street he still shared a bed with her best friend; Sarah would watch him fake cordial conversations with her son and husband. He might smile a knowing smile at her, tempting her to be stronger than he believed she was capable of being.

These thoughts carried her through the darkness, across the road, and beside his beat-up Ford pick-up truck. Her heart stabbed against her chest; the pumping became sharp daggers warning her of the vulnerability of life. Sarah began to balance herself against the hood before pulling back; the prints of her hands would remain momentarily before fading with time. She found herself staring at her hands holding the weapon, her age showing through; the rings encircled her fingers for so long now that a permanent indent remained. The rings were not embedded but curved as if her fingers willingly allowed the constraints they brought and molded to it. They told of her lifetime, as they decided her future.

She kneeled against the rough stones; her knees screamed at her to stand and run. She turned on the tiny flashlight she had left by her door and searched for the line that supplied the fluid giving it life. Her hands trembled as she touched the tube that became flesh in her hand, the skin she had wanted to scar as it hovered above her weeks before. It made it easier to make the slice, a slice that would cut through so many things.

MARY

Mary couldn't quite explain the unsettled feelings that rose her from her sleep that night. She went to the kitchen for a glass of water, hoping to settle her mind. Out of the corner of her eye, Mary saw a movement. She thought maybe it was a deer or stray dog, but as she pulled the curtain to the side, she saw Sarah creeping up their driveway. She couldn't exactly tell what she was doing but could tell she was trying to avoid watchful eyes.

Sarah disappeared between the cars for what seemed a long time. Mary considered going out to check on her, but before she headed to the door, Sarah's head reappeared. She was looking every which way and then very quickly, she darted across the road. Mary let the curtain fall back in place as if it had never moved at all.

CHAPTER 20
1 9 9 2
S a r a h

Sarah was surprised that when she opened her eyes, the sun was still shining, and she could hear the birds through the window. Nothing had changed in the world, or maybe the world was just unaware that the border between good and evil had blurred so that nothing would ever be the same.

She laid in bed and heard the clanging of dishes as Andy attempted to get breakfast ready. They had let her sleep. She sat up and rested on the side of the bed, testing what was real. Slowly, she slipped on her slippers and headed for the kitchen, trying hard to tell herself everything was normal. Somewhere in the corners of her mind, she heard a voice calling to her that it was not too late, she could admit to this. She could tell Andy what she had done and why, but then what would he do? All the original problems would come back. No, she told herself, what's done is done. She needed to stick to her plan.

Kyle came out of his bedroom when he smelled the eggs and toast. Andy poured him the coffee they had now accepted as his habit. Andy turned with the frying pan full of scrambled eggs ready to fill the next plate and noticed Sarah watching him.

"Good morning, sleepy."

She smiled at her husband. "I'm sorry. I just didn't sleep well last night."

"Quite all right. Would you like some eggs?"

"Sounds great," she lied.

They sat at the table in yet another uncomfortable silence. Sarah knew Kyle had a hard time looking at her. She realized the idea of something like this happening to a child's mother would be difficult. If it hadn't been a rape, then she believed he would be able to look her in the eyes, but it was just too hard.

Sarah could only stop and stare at the beauty of her two men, two men that were hurting so much because of something she had set in motion. Again, she told herself that if it were not meant to be, then Dan would end up fine. As if God was anywhere in her plan. As if one could test God that way.

Kyle wore blue jeans and a t-shirt that would be covered by the garage's overalls once he got to work. He knew that pumping gas and helping with oil changes was not glamorous or intellectually challenging. Despite this fact, he did it with abundant pride. Sometimes, looking at him made Sarah overcome with happiness. She would settle with the small piece of comfort her mind could muster.

"I decided to take the morning off and hang out with my wife. That okay with you, Sarah?" Andy asked.

"Please don't feel like you need to miss work for me."

"It's just the morning, and Kyle is going to help cover some of the work for me."

"Yeah, I should probably get going."

They all stood and set their plates on the counter where Sarah began cleaning them off. Andy started toward the door, talking shop with Kyle. She heard a pause in the conversation and looked up to see Kyle headed her way. Without a word, he wrapped his arms around his mother and held her. Letting go of her, he could only say, "I love you, Mom."

"I love you too, Kyle."

He caught up with his father and reminded him of the problems he was having with his starter.

"I thought you brought that in last weekend."

"Sorry, Dad. I ended up having plans with Scott and, well anyway, it hasn't been fixed."

"I'll take a look at it today."

Sarah half-listened as the conversation faded out the door. In the corner, she noticed her fern struggling with its last bit of hope for survival. Walking to the sink, wondering how she had let her healthy thriving plant whither right before her eyes, she heard Kyle's car struggle to turn over. It was a sound she had become accustomed to through the past weeks, and it landed on ears numb to the world around her. Again, the distant sound of the engine struggling to find life screamed to her silent ears, "Wake up, Sarah! Wake up!" She would forever ask herself why she wasn't listening. She poured the lukewarm water into the dry dirt around the plant and watched as two brown and shriveled leaves fell to the floor. She would pick them up later.

She became lost, not in thought, but in nothingness, because it was a comfortable place to be. Her hands mindlessly scrubbed the dishes and placed them on the drying rack. One plate at a time, as if she were a robot going through the motions. There was nothing behind her actions except for the need for the task to be completed.

As the glass in her hand slowly moved toward the drying rack, she heard tires desperately screeching, following by the distant but distinctive sound of metal on metal. Then there was the worst sound of all, a sound she had never heard before, the sound of her husband's scream. It was the sound that had reached across the boundaries, begging every soul in misery to cry out with it. It came to her slowly at first, and then the clear sound of Kyle's name cut through the walls. It was Andy's voice, yet a voice she could hardly recognize.

The glass dropped from her hand, and she found herself running, panicked and crying from a depth she did not know she had. Sarah saw Andy a hundred yards ahead of her, heading toward the stop sign at the bottom of the hill. And then she saw it. Dan's truck, severely damaged, another vehicle joined with it in a tangle of metal. The driver's side was nonexistent. It was somehow more real, more tragic than she had imagined. But there was something more than the accident, something more desperate behind Andy's scream, something a part of her brain already knew.

She raced toward the sound, her head scrambling, how, how did this happen? Why is Andy yelling Kyle's name? Kyle couldn't be in the truck. Kyle never rode with Dan. Why? Why today? Her mind raced at a speed that only her heart could keep pace with.

She could see Andy reaching the passenger side of the truck. She could see a figure, a silhouette in the rubble. Why was Andy saying Kyle's name? Why would Kyle be in Dan's truck? Her mind raced back in time to his car not starting easily, to Andy saying he would look at it later, the fragmented conversation she didn't pay enough attention to earlier. What did they say?

Prayers without words shot up to the heavens and were met only by her husband's voice, the sound of pure agony, screaming no, no. She began to hear herself screaming Kyle's name as she closed in on the truck. The distance was becoming less and less. Andy must have heard her too. He came toward her with such velocity knocking her breath from her as he tackled her in her tracks.

"No, Sarah, don't go. Please trust me."

Tears poured down his cheeks, and Sarah collapsed in his arms, sobbing. Life changed at that moment. She had gone from victim, to revenger, to murderer. All the faces, the faces of all the people she destroyed, stared down at her. Andy, he would never love her again; Amanda, her sweet Amanda, she could never face her; Mary, her best friend, she did this to her family. But most of all, Kyle, she took everything from him. There would be no more shared baseball moments, no evenings on the back porch with Andy, no petty, loving fights with his sister who adored him. She had disgraced all that was good in her life. She had destroyed everything. She felt herself slipping away at that moment to a place so dark it would be nearly impossible to escape. For reasons so evident to her, it felt comforting, like the darkness was the only place she would ever truly be able to fit into again, and she ran to it for comfort and acceptance.

Sarah stood next to Andy at the funeral. Neither of them was able to speak as the progression of people shook their hands and offered their condolences. Both Andy and Sarah were as empty as the casket was full, full of so much of their lives.

As the line of people tapered off, they were able to sit next to Amanda, who not being able to hear the uncomfortable condolences, sat alone. Andy sat between them and reached for both their hands. Sarah's hand settled into his but felt as limp and lifeless as the corpse of her only son. The next day they would attend Dan's funeral, and Sarah would find herself reaching for the hands of the daughters of the man she murdered. She could never tell them how sorry she genuinely was for her sins. She knew she could never be remorseful enough to make this right.

MARY

There is a difference between our secret hopes and reality. Mary realized that difference with each handshake. Her mouth stood stiff as her mind spoke for her, "What have I done?"

As everyone slowly recovered from such a tragic accident in a small town, they began to realize they had not heard of another rape. Lives went on in most homes as usual. Dinners were made, homework was completed, and closets that Mary had not seen the back of in years were cleaned out. Suits were donated, old work boots were tossed, and personal items discarded.

Months later, some kids found a bag full of the stolen items at the bottom of their swimming hole.

They assumed the rapist had decided it was time to move on to another defenseless town. Mary knew better.

ANDY

Andy stared up into the night sky, looking for answers between the stars. There were no answers, or at least the stars did not speak his language. Sarah was inside, asleep, most likely. She had gone into the bedroom after he had lost his temper and threw the ashtray against the wall. He knew he should have apologized. He even knew that he probably had frightened her. Hell, he terrified himself. It was the first time he had ever become violent like that.

He inhaled deeply, hoping the nicotine would calm him, and let it out slowly. He considered comforting Sarah, but he couldn't. He couldn't because it was entirely impossible for her to feel comforted. Every part of her had come under attack. Andy thought that nothing could ever be worse than finding out that someone had broken into his home and raped his wife. But then they didn't break-in, did they? The attacker had walked in through an unlocked door.

Neither one of them had even begun to heal from the rape before the accident happened. Andy wasn't even sure he was feeling the full extent of the pain yet. Nature had a distinctive way of helping people survive. He was numb. He would lay in bed, unable to comprehend why something so horrific would happen when they had just been through something so tragic.

That morning, he had woken up determined to find answers, determined that God could not possibly be so cruel. He slipped out of bed, threw on a jacket, and locked the door behind him. Andy knew where the officials took the car after the accident. He had to see it. He had to understand.

He found it thrown in a parking lot of tragic moments. Theirs was just another accident, another unfortunate event. He stared at it for many moments as he built up his courage, courage to confront the very demon that took his son. Slowly, he walked up to it and ran his hand over the jagged edges of the destroyed hood. Why didn't Dan stop? He avoided looking inside, far too afraid of what he might see.

Like a beaten old man, he lowered himself so that he could shimmy himself under the remains. One side of the truck tilted upward in such a way that it was as if it was trying to expose its secrets. Andy's body, directed by forces he could not explain, found himself staring up at the brake line. All his energy became absorbed into the ground, and he lay like a shell.

There were obvious marks on the brake line. Someone had cut it. He breathed slowly letting the clues piece together in his mind. He thought of

Sarah under the car, watching him change the brake line, wanting answers to questions she had never cared about before. But why? Andy felt a tear trickle down his face. There was only one reason.

Before he left that day, the evidence would not exist just in case someday, someone else began to wonder why. He couldn't comfort Sarah because he knew that, for now, they were both ruined. He couldn't comfort Sarah because, for now, he couldn't figure out what feeling was stronger, love or hate.

SARAH--PRESENT

As Sarah sat in her chair, she looked down at her wrinkled hands. The hands of a woman in her sixties that felt ancient and crippled. Every age spot told a story of days at the park, of scrubbing out stains, of catching baseballs and changing diapers, of drying tears and bandaging cuts, of holding hands and holding on.

It had been so many years since the day she said goodbye to her only son, but sometimes she could still feel the pain as if it were just happening. She thought about Andy and Kyle. Are they playing catch in heaven? Does Kyle get to hit a home run whenever he wishes for it? She wanted to be there, but instead, she could only stand at the cliff staring at the waters that were not yet welcoming. Her feet were still planted firmly to a rock that held nothing for her except pain and regret.

She wanted to close her eyes and see the smooth, even skin of her young hands. She wanted to feel the ball landing in her glove and see the sweet smile of her son. That was heaven to her. It was everything she once had without the worry of losing it again. Sarah was drawn back to reality as Drew Carey began calling the next contestant. She felt the wetness on her cheeks. After all these years, the old wound split open so easily.

CHAPTER 21

Amanda

The funeral was very difficult for Amanda. The town she used to love dripped despair and darkness onto its residence. First, her mother was raped right in their home and now... She could not allow the words to form. Her brother meant so much to her. As with most brothers, Kyle would pick at her, but through time, she realized he half did it to show affection and only half to annoy her. They understood each other. She even thought that he might follow her to Virginia Tech in another year.

She had to admit that she distanced herself at first. It was too hard to talk to her parents and to hear the sadness in their voices, especially her father's voice. The same blankness that she saw in her mother's eyes on her last visit was even worse. After a couple of months, her phone calls became more regular, and she even began sending her mother books again. They had always been able to discuss books, and Amanda hoped it would help get her talking again. Instead, her mother said she stopped reading. Sarah would apologize and say she was just too tired lately. She wouldn't even say she would try to read the next one. Amanda refused to give up.

She got a job with the school paper and knew her mother would be excited for her, or at least her old mother would have been. She sent home every article hoping for a response, but her mother never called. Every Sunday, Amanda would call her parents, and her father was almost himself. She knew this was most likely an act, but it still felt good to hear his voice returning. He would put Sarah on the phone at the end of their conversation, and she would listen politely while Amanda almost nervously chattered on. When she would respond, it was only short and empty comments. Amanda was beginning to realize it would never be the same.

SARAH

It was only months before Amanda showed signs of normalcy, but she would not know how hurtful that time was to Sarah. It took only the first few weeks for Sarah to decide she was unworthy of her daughter's love, and she shut down.

The books continued to come in the mail sporadically, even if the book talks didn't follow. Amanda always included a letter about what she was learning and friends she was meeting. She wrote her letters to stay close to her parents. Sarah knew this but could only imagine it was out of obligation. Instead of bringing her closer, her letters made Sarah feel abandoned. She had lost both her children. When the phone calls started to come again, and Amanda started visiting again, Sarah was already cold and distant.

When Amanda visited, she would sit out on the back porch with Andy overlooking their memories. Maybe they were able to talk about Kyle, but Sarah felt she had no right to be a part of their conversation. She would glance at them through the window occasionally. The sight of them together made her feel left out. The open invitation to join them fell on deaf ears.

She never told Amanda that she continued to read every book she ever sent her. She became a castaway in Amanda's journey in life because she knew her own life was over. The books were impersonal enough that they didn't intimidate her like her letters, but now and then she would picture their book talks, and she would miss them.

Most evenings, Sarah and Andy sat in the living room where the dust-covered unopened curtains and piles of magazines advertising sales that she would never care about lay scattered. Sarah would stare at a blank piece of paper, thinking about what she would say to her only living child. Whatever she tried to write always came out so cold and so meaningless that she left the paper untouched. Trying to say I love you was a betrayal on her lips.

Her secrets made the words burn like acid, so she stopped saying them at all.

She could tell Amanda she was making beef stew, but the magic Sarah had once found in cooking had fizzled to nothingness. She saw her words through her daughter's eyes and felt her life had become meaningless. Food became less of an act of love than a fulfilling of an inner void, and Sarah found herself gaining weight and not caring. Her once womanly figure disappeared, much like everything else that she once knew to be herself. She was a shell echoing her secrets repeatedly, vibrating her soul with self-hatred.

Andy would still come home for lunch. Sarah set up their television trays and prepared their sandwiches. Sometimes it would be tuna, sometimes BLT's, sometimes grilled cheese. She alternated, searching for the flavor she remembered but could not find it. Sometimes she thought she could rediscover it if she ate a second one, but somehow this made her feel more lost.

It had many months of somberness in their home when Andy came home for lunch, sat in his chair, and routinely thanked Sarah for lunch, and she routinely said thank you. They sat in silence, chewing, swallowing and watching. *The Price is Right* began at its regular time, and they watched without thought. Bob Barker called the next contestant, and the contestant jumped from her seat with an excitement that was alien to Sarah. She ran down the aisle jumping and squealing until her halter top shockingly fell, exposing her breasts to the world.

That was the moment when Sarah and Andy both stopped chewing and stared at the screen, and then a sound came that ripped through the silence. Andy laughed. It was the most incredible sound that Sarah had heard in so long that she felt a chuckle sneak from her throat. In a moment, they were both laughing harder than the occasion called for, and for the first time in months, the wetness on their cheeks wasn't from sadness. Laughter amid despair was like a waterfall for the parched, and she wanted to dance in it, if just for that moment.

Sarah began joining Andy on the porch again. They would light their cigarettes, and the smoke would create halos encircling them both. Sometimes they would talk about their days, and sometimes they would sit in silence. Those were the moments when they could still feel their shattered souls, the moments that no words existed to express.

In one of those moments, she heard Andy's rocking chair slide toward hers and felt Andy's hand move to hold hers. She tried to stop her mind from thinking of the things her hand had done and lost herself in the courageous warmth that she had loved from the very first day she held him. From that night on, Andy would reach for her hand and hold it as the smoke swirled, and the stars looked over them. The quiet drift through life had begun and would take her to the very end of his existence.

CHAPTER 22

Sarah

Sarah never missed going to visit her son's grave every Sunday. She and Andy would leave the church, stop by the local farmer's market for flowers, and bring them to the gravesite. Sarah wondered why bringing something that still held a bit of life in it to a place full of death became so important. Maybe she was letting her son know his memory was still alive. Most Sundays, she found it hard to look at the grave as if she was making eye contact with Kyle, and he would be able to read all her secrets.

Occasionally, Andy would go alone during the week. It was on those days he was the quietest, and Sarah suspected he knew he would not be able to control his emotions. Somehow, he still believed it would appear weak to cry in front of his wife. All Sarah knew was that she would be too weak to witness it.

On other occasions, Sarah would visit the cemetery with Mary, and very occasionally, Mary's girls would join them. It was a painfully hot Sunday, and Andy was feeling run down. He had been sleeping in more, and he often appeared to be fighting a cold. Sarah couldn't help but notice how much Andy had aged. Now in his fifties, he was completely gray, and even through his smile, he looked more worn. Sarah was surprised when he skipped church to rest but not worried. She had learned to enjoy her alone time.

As Sarah opened her car door, she heard Mary approaching.

"Morning, Sarah. You off to church without Andy?"

"He just can't kick this cold. I'm sure with a good day's rest, he'll be feeling better." Sarah detected a look in Mary's eyes, a look of knowing concern.

"He needs to cut down his hours at the garage. He's not thirty anymore."

"I'll let him know you said that. Now I need to get to church."

"Are you going to the cemetery after?"

"Don't I always?"

"The girls are coming in for brunch this afternoon. How 'bout we join you and go to brunch from there?" Sarah knew better than to argue with her, so she quickly agreed and drove off, annoyed. Mary kept trying to pull her back into a world she was trying to avoid, a world she did not deserve.

Sarah and Mary parked in front of the cemetery with Mary's daughters. They walked hand in hand, a united front against the pain and suffering of their past. The metal fence that separated the world from these spirits stood as hundreds of soldiers, tall and strong, never bending or slacking in their job. As much as she wanted to push Mary's girls away just like everyone else, she couldn't. They were Sarah's family but even better; they never expected anything from her.

A breeze came from nowhere, and for a moment, Sarah couldn't breathe. It was a silent threat that she too was but a vulnerable human easily taken out with the small slice of a knife, the very breath she depended on could be blown out of her in an instant. They walked together over grass that crunched under their feet, a sign that the intense summer sun was bearing down, and not all would survive.

"We'll meet you back up front," Mary's voice announced their separation, and Eva's hand slipped out of hers. Sarah watched them walk away for a moment, all three of them with their backs to her, and she turned toward the grave of her son. Kyle and Dan were buried in the same cemetery but on different sides. Sarah had chosen this. She said it was to allow them some privacy, but in some way, she felt she was protecting Kyle from a monster.

There was but one cloud in the sky, and it found the sun as she approached. The black-eyed Susans slumped in her hand, and she tried to stand them erect against the headstone. She brushed her hand across the gray slab marking her son's life as if she were brushing away the bangs from his sweet face, a face she struggled to remember. The cold and unwelcoming sensation spread throughout her body and settled in her heart. She pulled her shaking hand away. In every way possible, he had left her.

Sarah could see the three of them in the distance. She could see them raising tissues to their overflowing eyes. The wind whispered through the trees, and a crow shouted out her secret. But Mary and her children could not hear the echo of guilt that rang through her ears.

Sarah had never joined them on the other side before, but the breeze summoned her to hear her verdict. Her legs carried her closer to them as she studied their faces, faces mourning a man they never truly knew. Didn't they realize they were better off?

Sarah stood about ten feet from the gravesite, a closeness she had never reached before. As if from another person, words slid from her mouth. "I wonder where we would all be if it weren't for that day."

Mary thought for a moment, "That is something we will never know, now will we?"

Sarah's head shot up, and she tried to catch on Mary's face what she was sure was in her words, an accusation, but just as quickly as it appeared, it was gone.

Mary put an arm around each daughter, and they headed for the gate.

"I'll come in a bit," Sarah replied to the invitation that they hadn't spoken.

"Okay."

She stood alone with Dan for the first time since the day he raped her. Although this time, Dan was only a corpse with his gray suit clinging to his decayed body. Sarah fell to her knees, allowing each blade of dried grass to cut at her bare legs reaching out to grab her and leave their mark. She had done this. She was responsible for these horrors. Each tear that the three women had shed was on her.

Sarah could only whisper at first, testing the power of her words, "I'm sorry, Dan." In a tree, a crow screamed again. "I'm sorry."

She buried her face in her hands and cried as the winds swirled around her in a gust, separating her sins from Dan's. They became two separate entities, his choices and hers, both equal, both evil. As she stood over Dan's remains, she began to see him as a whole person. At one point, he was a young boy growing up without role models; he was a husband to her best friend. There had to have been some good moments between them. Hadn't she seen the girls rush to his truck with open arms? She assumed his smile was only a cover for his wrongdoings, but maybe there was love there, too.

She had cut his journey short, and they would never know what God had in store for Dan. What lessons did he still need to learn, this husband, father, and yes, rapist? Sarah had always figured that there would be nothing good in him or for the people whose lives he touched. What if she was wrong? What if by some slight chance Mary did end up rescuing him from the dark before Dan dragged her in with him? Somewhere in the distance, she heard the gavel of the judge and the resounding words guilty, guilty, guilty.

MARY

Mary sat in the car, watching Sarah, and could only imagine the conversation she was having with her dead husband. She heard the sniffling of her girls as they consoled each other in the back seat. Mary was the strong one. She had always been the strong one. How did she fail so many people? Somewhere in Dan was the child lost in the darkness. He was above her, calling to her. Like so many baby animals she had tried in vain to save, he was too far gone when she found him. Her girls, without him they would not exist, but with him, they had no role model of a husband and a father. They would never understand how short he fell. She could only hope that they came across a less hopeless creature to take as their own.

She watched Sarah as she became a corpse of a person right in front of her. Mary had never felt as useless. She knew from being a nurse that no matter how many gadgets a doctor might own, nothing could save a person if they had no will to survive. Mary knew that no matter what words she chose to say to her friend, they would not change anything. Worse yet, she feared the wrong ones might destroy her. Mary swore to herself that she would stay by her friend until Sarah found her way out of the darkness. If she needed to, she would walk through hell with her friend until she could see the sunshine. She would do this no matter how long it took.

CHAPTER 23

Amanda

Amanda should have known something was wrong the minute she picked up the phone. Her mother never called, and although she tried to be patient with her moods sometimes, she couldn't help but feel angry. A switch had been shut off the day she was raped or maybe before that.

It had been years since she lost her brother, still, nothing had returned to normal. Her thoughts drifted back to the first time that she sensed a season of her life was coming to an end. It was that weekend, the one her mother acted so strangely. Shortly after, her mother was attacked. Amanda could not shake the feeling that everything was connected.

She knew her mother would battle with many feelings after the rape, but she believed, at the time, that she would win in the end. She had such a loving family and such a steadfast best friend next door. Unfortunately, before Sarah could even begin to heal from one tragedy, Kyle died. It was almost as if someone wanted her to fall off a cliff.

She felt angry with fate, with her mother, with everything. Her trips back home were only bearable because of her father. She loved sitting outside with him. She would rest her head on his shoulder, and he would assure her everything would be all right. Her father always made her feel safe, but even his words weren't as confident as they used to be. He was tired. Everyone could feel it.

"Hello, Amanda. It's Mom."

"Hi. I'm surprised to..."

"Listen, Amanda, I think you should come home."

Amanda's heart dropped. How much more could she take? "Why? What's wrong?"

"It's your father. I'm sorry to tell you this, but the doctor told us he has lung cancer. It would mean a lot to him to see you right now."

"I'll be there as quickly as I can. Can I talk to him?"

"He's resting right now. I'd rather not wake him."

"No, please don't. Tell him I love him, and I'll be there very soon."

"Thank you, Amanda. I'm glad you're coming."

Amanda was immediately on the phone booking plane tickets and explaining to Nick why she was flying home. She had been dating Nick for some time, and he had proposed a couple of times already. Amanda just couldn't say yes yet. She had to fill her holes before she could decide who was right for her.

Nick was perfect, though, and she knew the problem was her own. He was also a writer and taught classes at a local college as his full-time job. He was amazingly patient with her. When she pushed away, he let her. He seemed to understand. He would get lost in his world of literature and be there for her when she came around to accepting him. There were times he practically lived with her and then times when they would go days without talking. Sometimes on the back porch, Amanda would tell Andy all about him, and he would listen quietly. One night he finally asked the obvious question.

"What's holding you back, Amanda? You sound like you love him, and it sounds like he's good to you."

"Maybe marriage isn't for me, Dad. What if...what if I end up really unhappy or what if I make him unhappy? I just feel like I'm trying to figure it all out, and I don't want to be a burden on anyone."

Andy sat silent for some time before speaking. "Do you think your mother is a burden on me?"

"I didn't say that. It's just that Mom hasn't been herself for so long that I don't even know who that other person was anymore."

Andy paused thoughtfully. "Life has been hard on your mother. Harder than we may ever understand, but she's never been a burden to me." Andy took Amanda's hand. "But that's what makes marriage beautiful, Amanda. When life makes you so lost that you can't find the surface anymore, you have a person that loves you through all of it. If you marry the right person, you may take turns being the anchor, but someone is always on the surface, reminding you it's there. I believe your mom will find the surface again, and I hope to be there when she does."

Amanda had to step away, to try to absorb all her father was trying to teach her. She went for a walk to the nearby park where she once played long before life turned dark. When she returned, her father was asleep in the recliner, his skin was ashen, and she knew. Her father would not live long enough to help her mother resurface, and a bit of anger rose in her knowing that her mother would continue to be an anchor, refusing to come up for air.

SARAH

Amanda came home often as Andy continued to decline. At Andy's request, she brought Nick with her on several of the trips. Sarah would cook dinner and spend time in the kitchen with Amanda while the men got to know each other. She wanted to speak to Amanda like she used to, but nothing felt natural. Sarah would ask questions about Nick like a mother was supposed to, but somehow, the attempts at conversation even sounded hollow to herself. Inside Sarah knew she had lost the title of mother due to unworthiness, and intimate questions were not her right.

What Sarah enjoyed most was when Mary came over to join them in the kitchen. Mary still played the mother role so easily, and Sarah could live vicariously through her friend as Mary led her into the secrets of her daughter's life. Sarah decided that Nick seemed perfect, and she wanted to scream at her daughter, *Marry him. Don't let him go!*

It was Andy's influence that finally swayed Amanda. Sarah helped Amanda get ready quietly, watching her daughter's reflection as she pinned her hair on top of her head. Amanda avoided eye contact, and Sarah physically felt nauseated by the rejection she knew she deserved. Almost by accident, their eyes locked for a moment, and just for the time it took to let out their breaths, they saw each other. Sarah knew the shield had dissolved for just a horrifying instant. Amanda looked away first, and Sarah felt words come from her as miraculously as words from a mute.

"I love you, Amanda," Amanda responded with silent tears that she quickly wiped away.

AMANDA

Getting married terrified Amanda, but what she could not comprehend was a wedding without her father. She knew how special it would be to hold his arm and stand proudly next to a man strong enough to be the pillar through it all. Some families she found only had one. How could she not give her father the moment he had dreamed of when she knew his time was limited?

After the wedding, things progressed rapidly. Amanda watched as her mother ran around the house frantically trying to care for her dying husband, looking a bit like someone trying to wipe up a gallon of spilled milk with a tissue. Her mother's rare softness at the wedding was a surprise that felt more confusing than comforting. Now that the wedding day was over, they were back to being two strangers battling their demons alone. The physically closer they became, the farther apart she felt.

At night, when all the Hospice nurses had left, Amanda or Sarah would sit with Andy while he fell asleep. They moved a television into the bedroom, a final step to him spending the rest of his days confined to a small space. She was there the night her father died. It was her mother's turn to sit beside him as he fell asleep for the night. She had been in there for quite some time before Amanda began to hear her quiet sobs. The idea of facing her mother when she came out of the bedroom was too much. She grabbed her jacket and got in the car to drive anywhere the car would take her.

SARAH

She knew the moment was coming and couldn't stop it. She had to tell Andy; he had to know her sins. Her mind raced frantically. If she told him and the last expression that she saw on his face was hatred, she would die with him. She couldn't stand the thought. Her mind whirled around options so fast that her eyes couldn't focus. She felt Andy's hand on hers, and she looked into his glossy eyes.

"Promise me you'll find your happiness."

She prayed she wasn't lying, and she whispered,

"I will."

"Thank you." As Andy began to fade, Sarah held onto his hand with a hand now stronger than his.

"Tell Kyle, I love him," she felt his hand go completely limp, "and that I'm sorry."

AMANDA--2002-PRESENT

After her father's funeral, months went by before Amanda called Sarah again. She didn't want to admit how much she needed her mother, but she desperately did. With her father and brother gone, her mother was the last remaining piece of the base from which her life sprung. Without her, Amanda felt she was floating in the world around her, never knowing where to place herself.

The phone calls were as cold as expected, far too cold to put herself through often, so she did what she did best; she wrote. She wrote about everything; date nights with Nick, how he wanted to start a family, and what window treatments she bought for her small home. She even told her she would love her to come to visit, knowing she would never step foot on a plane. She would send her the latest novel she read and invite her to call or write; she was almost begging for their old book talks. She did this, also knowing a response would never come.

She reverted to calling Mary, a woman that had always been so easy to talk to, to find out how her mother was doing. She began to form a new closeness with her, and Amanda completely understood why her mother loved her. She knew how to make things airy and comfortable, no matter how much shadow her mother could cast. Mary made her believe that there was hope for Sarah, who had been in a bad mood for so long it could no longer honestly be considered a mood. Through Mary and maturity, Sarah became less of an ache than a quest. She would find her mother again, even if it took decades.

CHAPTER 24
Present
Sarah

Riding home from Dr. Chamber's office was somber. Sarah wondered how it felt to be Mary, to have to watch a lifelong friend die, to hear they had only months left together at best. Had the past years of deterioration prepared Mary? Could she be wishing it was over so that her duties could be relinquished? As Sarah sat in her chair at home, breathless from the effort of breathing, she knew her time was quickly approaching, but hearing the doctor's words made everything too real.

Sarah thought back to that summer when Andy's bad cold quickly progressed to something much worse. By September, the doctors were preparing Sarah that the man she had loved for most of her life was dying of lung cancer. It was as if by speaking the words, it caused reality to spill over the dam at an unstoppable pace. His death gave her life, but only because she so desperately tried to be strong for him, something she had never had to do. Yes, she tried to act strong after the rape, but Kyle's death came so quickly that she was knocked off her stumbling feet and would not get up again.

She thought about the preparations she had to go through for the funeral and knew she could not leave this for Mary. Despite this fact, somewhere inside of her, was a child forced to go to summer camp with no bug spray or sunscreen. She was unprotected from the fate she would meet. She felt frozen with fear and ignorance. How does someone prepare themselves for death? She looked over at Mary confidently, sitting behind the wheel, and prayed for direction.

MARY

Mary opened her windows for the first time that spring day. She glanced around her yard and could imagine where she would plant each pansy, where each bulb from the past would peek through the moist spring soil. Mary loved spring. Her sheets were already on the line, and she couldn't wait to nestle into them when the day was over. Before that could happen, she would do what she had done every Sunday for the past few years. She would take Sarah to church.

Sarah, Mary suspected, pretended to listen attentively only to return home where the demons inside her mind would fight for control. Mary enjoyed seeing everyone every week. She enjoyed the picnics afterward, and occasionally she even let herself be lost in the priest's homily. Most of all, she liked seeing her friend get out of her ratty nightgown and brush her hair.

Life had been hard on both women. What made Mary crazy was that for all Sarah proclaimed about God and religion, she had thrown herself into a self-inflicted purgatory. From everything Mary heard, when she was listening, was that only God could send someone there. Despite this, Sarah seemed to relish in her solitary sentence. Since Mary felt responsible, she swam through the muck with her.

Mary let the spring air swim around her for a moment longer before going back into the dark with her friend. Purse in hand, she practiced her best smile and headed for the door. Time was limited. She needed to find the answer.

Sarah had managed to slip into her best dress that Mary had laid out for her the night before. She had brushed her hair into a slick gray crown. Lipstick almost covered her lips in the right places. Mary smiled and thought that if only Sarah had half the sense of humor she once had; she would get a good laugh at the wrinkled woman trying to slip into her outdated shoe.

"Well, now aren't you the pretty one today," Mary said optimistically.

"Do I sense sarcasm?"

"Sarcasm? I'm not familiar with that term," Mary said with a smile. Sarah had a wheelchair she used for her rare outings, and Mary pulled it up alongside the bed and waited. Sarah looked at her expectantly.

"My dear friend, I think we have given up trying altogether."

"Fine, I'll do it but if I fall on the floor don't blame me if you mess your hair trying to get me up."

Mary rolled her eyes and walked to her side. "Have you ever heard of shaken elderly syndrome?"

"What?"

"Never mind. Just a passing thought."

Mary thought back to all the times with her children that had tried her very soul. Her love for her friend was disturbingly similar at times. How much she needed a break some days, but she would also always have unconditional love for her.

Mary wheeled Sarah's chair down the aisle as she waved and smiled at the familiar faces. Sarah lifted her palm an inch from the armrest, which Mary felt symbolized how much she cared for any of them. She parked her next to the pew and took her seat. White lilies decorated the altar. Mary knew that was another symbol, but she just thought they were beautiful signs of spring.

Mary's mind wandered as the first reading, a song, and the second reading were, in her mind, monotonously and routinely performed. She thought back to the many times she had joined Sarah and her father for Sunday's service. Even if she didn't understand everything they got out of it, she enjoyed going with them. Maybe it was the act of putting on their Sunday best or the calmness on people's faces she observed while people-watching. Perhaps it was something she would never understand.

Father Argy began the Gospel reading of the day which would generally give Mary more time to ponder her upcoming plans or check out the latest fashions being worn, but for some reason, her attention was drawn to the sound of his voice.

"A reading from the Gospel of Mark 2:1-2:12. And again he entered into Capernaum after some days; it was noised that he was in the house. And straightway many were gathered together, insomuch that there was no room to receive them, no, not so much as about the door: and he preached the word unto them. And they come unto him, bringing one sick of the palsy, which was borne of four. And when they could not come nigh unto him for the press, they uncovered the roof where he was: and when they had broken it up, they let down the bed wherein the sick of the palsy lay."

When Jesus saw their faith, he said unto the sick of the palsy, Son, thy sins be forgiven thee. But there was certain of the scribes sitting there, and reasoning in their hearts. Why doth this man thus speak blasphemies? Who can forgive sins but God only? And immediately when Jesus perceived in his spirit that they so reasoned within themselves, he said unto them, Why reason ye these things in your hearts? Whether is it easier to say to the sick of the palsy, Thy sins be forgiven thee; or to say, Arise and take thy bed, and walk? But that ye may know that the Son of man hath power on earth to forgive sins, (he saith to the sick of the palsy,) I say unto thee, Arise, and take up thy bed, and go thee way into thine house. And immediately he arose, took up the bed, and went forth before them all; insomuch that they were all amazed, and glorified God, saying. We never saw it on this fashion." Mark 2:12 King James Version (KJV)

Mary looked at her friend, who appeared to be following along only blindly. She realized that Sarah was as much paralyzed as the man on the mat and wondered to herself if she would ever hear the words 'Get up, take your mat and walk?'

Mary slowly pushed Sarah's wheelchair to the car, allowing herself time to embrace each conversation. Sarah kept her head down, avoiding as much as she could. Each person would politely address Sarah as well. She would greet them with the same small lift of her hand, intended to be a wave.

Father Argy was one of the last to address them. Mary generally tried to avoid him since she felt like an intruder in his place of worship, always questioning and never quite letting it make sense in her world.

"Well, hello, Mary and Sarah. It's always nice to see you each Sunday even if I only catch the back of your heads at the end of mass."

Mary thought maybe he could smell death, and like some kind of sin-vulture, knew it was time to swoop in and devour it before it was too late. What about him made Mary think that he could see straight through them?

"Hello, Father Argy. Sorry not to stop and chat. Sarah tires easily. I try to get her home at a decent time." Was it wrong to lie to the priest that just watched her joyously speak to everyone in her path?

"Oh, I understand. Sarah, if you get too tired to make it out, I can always make house calls. Just call the church, and I would be glad to visit with you."

Sarah thanked the priest while Mary nervously shifted from one foot to the other, anxiously trying to avoid his knowing eyes. With his help, Sarah was buckled in the passenger seat, and they were driving away. They sat in silence for a moment before Mary began to speak.

"So, what did you think of the Gospel today?" Mary asked.

Still a bit winded, Sarah said, "Gospel, well look at you, knowing the parts of the mass."

"How many years have I taken you? I had to have picked up something, right?"

Sarah thought for a moment. "I guess. I didn't really think much of anything."

"You didn't think anything. Why am I dragging your wheezy butt to church every Sunday if you're not even listening? One of us needs to be getting something out of it."

"I just feel like I should go. I guess it's just what I've always done."

Again, there was silence. "Well, let me tell you my ignorant understanding of the passage. It was about Jesus forgiving a paralyzed man, and once he forgave him, he told him to pick up his mat and walk away. And guess what, the man picked up his mat and walked away."

Sarah thought for a moment. "So, are you telling me that you now believe the stories in the Bible."

"Sarah, we think differently. I don't know what I believe. I think there's something more powerful than us that is at play in our lives. So, I guess, yes, I believe. But what I don't understand is how you have always claimed to be a Catholic. You used to read the Bible, and go to confession, and live the life of a Catholic. Then life changed. Now you go through the motions. You live with the guilt but not the forgiveness. You're like that paralyzed man."

"Maybe you don't know what you're talking about. You don't understand everything."

Mary searched herself for the right words, the only words she would allow herself to say. "I don't know everything that goes on inside your head, but

I do think that whatever religion or whatever spiritual belief you choose to have, it should be about helping you through life, lifting you up, giving you direction. It shouldn't destroy you. I may not be as good of a religious person as you are, but I'm happy. So maybe you're not really listening to what your religion is trying to tell you. God didn't put you here to be miserable."

"God didn't put me here to... Never mind. Just... Not everything here was God's idea."

Mary took a deep breath and tried to find the words as if she were speaking to a child. "Maybe not, Sarah, but the way I see it is that life is kind of like a big tie-dye shirt. It may have many different colors, some dark, some light, but when they swirl together, it's beautiful. Unless, of course, you keep mixing them together so much that you can't see the light colors through the dark. Then you're just swimming in some nasty brown. Just let the good lie where it lies, and the bad do the same. They aren't meant to wash each other out."

"How very poetic of you. And how do you suggest I do that?"

"I don't know, Sarah, but start by allowing some of the good memories back in without letting them send you into chronic depression. For God's sake, Sarah, there was a lot of good in your life. Do you know how many people would have given their left arm for a husband like Andy? He was devoted to you." Mary paused a moment, and then said, "I never had a day of that in my life with Dan. And Kyle... you loved that boy. You've erased everything that you loved. Amanda is sitting in front of you, begging for your attention, and you ignore her. Just stop, Sarah! We all have pain and regret. All of us. Stop being some martyr. Stop before it's too late."

Mary had to catch her breath. She had held back for too long. The silence that fell between them told her Sarah was listening. "Sarah, if you say you're living as a Catholic, then live as a Catholic. You've been taught as a Catholic how to help yourself, then help yourself the way Catholics do. Why don't you call Father Argy? You know whatever you say to him is just between the two of you."

Sarah spoke carefully. "What makes you so sure I have something to say?"

"Because I haven't seen you get up and 'walk' in a very long time. You pretend to live by the book, well, let me just say, I love you, but you can be a real downer sometimes."

"Well, thanks."

"I'm just saying, with all that love, peace, and forgiveness around, don't you think you'd be a bit happier? You're a bit of a mess, my friend."

Sarah looked out the side window for an answer, and instead, she found her reflection. For the first time, she noticed how her lipstick on one side was a good quarter inch above her lip. She tried to rub it off but only smeared it more. "Maybe I am a bit of a mess."

"Well, how bout we start finding something to smile about while we still can." Mary let an exaggerated smile reach across her face exposing the red lipstick smeared across her teeth. From somewhere inside Sarah that she no longer knew existed came a tiny but precious laugh, and a small chip of the shield fell away.

"That's the spirit."

CHAPTER 25

Decision 4
Present
Sarah

ary burst into Sarah's living room the next morning with an energy that, at first, intimidated Sarah. It was like watching a tidal wave sweeping across the ocean and knowing there was no choice but to be swept away with it. She tried to brace herself.

"I have a plan!"

"Great," Sarah mumbled in return.

"I've been up all night, thinking. So, you're dying. I'm losing my friend; you're losing your life. Both situations stink, right?"

"I fail to see the cause for excitement."

"What's new? Now, this is where it gets exciting. We're not going to think of it like that. You are going on a trip to see Andy and Kyle, and you are not taking that sour puss face of yours with you. They don't want to see it." Sarah could already feel the air shifting.

"We are not preparing for your death. We are preparing for the trip of your lifetime." Sarah's nature was to argue or use sarcasm, but her options were limited, and a plan to meet her husband and son sounded so much better than dying.

"Do you know what Andy made me promise him as he was before he passed? He made me promise I would find my happiness. I haven't found it yet."

"No offense, but I don't think you have ever looked. It's awfully hard to find your happiness when you're hiding under a rock." Sarah couldn't argue again.

"What's the big plan?"

"While first, you are going to do something with yourself. I have hair appointments for both of us this afternoon. You're getting rid of your premature grays and finding the brunette you once were." Sarah felt almost a giddiness rising in her. "Anything else you need done?"

"I haven't had a pedicure in a long time." Sarah thought she saw Mary smile up to Heaven at her words.

"I'll set that up. While we're out, we should probably grab some lunch, too, depending on how you're holding up, of course."

"Sounds great. What are your other life-changing plans?"

"You'll see, but since it's your trip, you should probably think of some things on your own."

"I may have some."

Sarah knew what she needed to do, and the excitement turned to panic. She also knew she would not hide from it anymore; there was no more time.

"The mission has begun. I'll be back at 11:00 for our spa day, so be ready."

"I will be."

Mary had given her the smallest thing, but it was something. A plan. Sarah's heart beat a bit faster, and she found herself counting down the minutes until Mary returned.

That night Sarah sat on the edge of her bed, admiring her toes. Pink of all colors. They reminded her of spring, so bright and cheery she almost didn't notice the wrinkled feet attached to them. She glanced up and caught her image in the mirror. A stranger she once knew smiled back at her, and there was beauty there. Mary was right about the hair color. Andy would love it.

MARY AND SARAH

Sarah sat, watching *The Price is Right* and waiting for Mary. She had called the night before to warn her that they would be going for a walk after lunch. Mary assured her that exercise was vital in preparation for the trip. Sarah wasn't quite sure how Mary pushing her in her wheelchair counted as a mutual workout, but she remained open-minded. It was time to become part of the world she had long forgotten.

Drew Carey brought the whole LA Dodgers team on *The Price Is Right*, and Sarah watched them through Andy's lost eyes. She could almost hear Andy's comments watching two of his pastimes come together. Most likely, he would have been wishing it were the Yankees instead.

The players presented Drew Carey with a jersey. Sarah thought of the many pieces of baseball attire that Andy brought home for Kyle throughout the years. He was born knowing baseball and very early could be heard commenting on the games as he sat next to his father on the couch decked out in matching baseball caps and jerseys.

She remembered how she would spend the time with Amanda and her new favorite baby doll. Just like her mother, Amanda seemed as if she were born to be a mother. Sarah sat with her and pretended to be Grandma throughout her imaginary play.

"Mommy, what should we name my baby?"

"Well, your Grandma's name was Louise."

"Mommy, she's not an old lady." Sarah laughed at her youthful honesty.

"Tell me a pretty name, Mommy."

As Sarah fastened the tiny buttons of the baby's dress, she heard the cheers coming from the other room. She could see them, together as always, and she had to smile.

"How about Elizabeth?"

"Oh, I love that name." Amanda took her baby from her and picked her up as if seeing her for the first time.

"That's what we'll name her." Sarah had tried to avoid her memories for so long, but she found that they were beginning to seep into her thoughts no matter how hard she fought them.

The quick knock and opening of the door brought Sarah back to the present.

"Are we ready for our walk?" Mary practically sang.

"If you insist."

"Well, now aren't we just a ball of excitement." Mary didn't skip a beat of enthusiasm and pushed the wheelchair over to her friend. "I thought we would head down to the park."

How many years had it been? Too many and not enough. Sarah immediately felt her heart begin to panic as she pictured the ghosts that lingered there. She tried to make eye contact with Mary to read into her intentions. What was she trying to accomplish by dragging her to that place? Mary knew how often Sarah had watched Amanda's bobbing ponytail as she raced around the playground or listened to the sounds of the bats making contact during the endless baseball games

Kyle played on the nearby field. Mary refused to look at her as she busied herself with the portable oxygen tank.

After a few long moments, they were on their way down the sidewalk. It had deteriorated some through the years, and Mary struggled to get the wheelchair over the larger bumps. Neither of them spoke for some time.

Sarah could feel herself begin to ease into their adventure. Warm spring air glided over her cheeks, and for the first time in forever, she heard the birds singing to ears that had been frozen for so long. The cherry trees were in bloom, and when Sarah let her eyes travel, she found an eruption of azalea blossoms lining the yards of many homes.

The sound of her voice surprised even herself. "Thank you, Mary."

Mary felt the tight pain in her throat, and she stifled the cry that threatened to escape. "Don't thank me. This is finally something I enjoy doing with you."

Sarah smiled but could not explain why. "You have been good to me," and in a rare moment of real honesty, "better than I deserve."

"Now don't be getting soft on me. We do for each other. We always have."

"And what is something I've done for you?"

Mary thought of the many things, but for now, she only said, "You taught me how to pray."

"Oh, really, I didn't know you pray."

"Damn right. Excuse me, I mean, I have to. I gave up on trying to fix you a long time ago. I had to call in the cavalry."

Sarah began to hear the laughter from the playground, and somewhere inside of her peace that she barely remembered tried to shimmy to the surface. She shook her head to clear it away.

"Well, you better keep praying for me, my half-hearted Catholic friend. I'm far from fixed."

"You should know better than to label me, Sarah." Mary paused a moment before continuing. "The way I see it, religions are like prom dresses. You may choose to wear the bulky one, and I may choose the flattering slender one, but they both get you to the dance."

"Interesting analogy," Sarah thought a moment, "but which one of us will be crowned prom queen?"

Mary let out a small laugh. "My bet would be neither one of us, Sarah."

Sarah smiled to herself, envisioning the two of them; flawed, bruised, and battered by life wearing their crooked crowns in heaven. "Mine, too."

Mary pushed Sarah's chair until she reached the bench. She parked beside it and sat quietly next to her friend. Mary thought of the many times they sat on a similar bench so many years before. She wanted so much for her friend to remember the good. There was so much of it. It's what carried Mary through all the bad. Why couldn't Sarah let it in, too?

"I think we should get going now," Sarah said with urgency.

"Easy for you to say. I just pushed you all the way here, and I'm gonna catch my breath a minute."

Sarah's head turned back and forth, and Mary wondered if it was to prevent her from truly looking at anything. A piercing scream cut through the air, and a young girl took off in a panicked run away from a barefoot muddy boy with something in his hand. The chase was interrupted by the two mothers, one apologizing for her son and one saying, "Rachel, it's just a crawfish. Calm down." Sarah's eyes opened, and she stared into the past.

"Do you remember..." Her voice caught her throat.

"Sarah, I never forgot."

Mary waited patiently in silence.

"Remember the storm?"

"Yes, I do."

Sarah struggled to let words of the past find their way to the surface.

"Andy always liked storms." Again, she paused. "We always sat on the porch every night and looked out over our yard. I don't even know what we were looking at half the time. When the kids were little, we watched them. So many times, I watched Andy and Kyle playing catch."

Mary found it hard to breathe, so afraid that if she did anything, she would stop her friend from talking. It had been so long since she had heard her say their names.

"They would play catch, and Amanda would sit on my lap. I used to love to nuzzle my nose into Amanda's hair and smell her shampoo. She smelled like spring, so clean and fresh."

A tear formed in Mary's eye, but she quickly brushed the evidence away.

"We sat out there almost every night after dinner. Do you remember how much we liked our back porch?"

"I remember."

Sarah let out a small laugh. "Except when it stormed. I never did like the storms. Andy would say, 'This rocking chair sits out here during every storm, and it's never been struck by lightning. What makes you think just because you're in it that it's gonna get struck?' He was probably right. Kyle was just like his dad. He would pull my rocking chair up next to him and ride out the storm with him. I can still picture them." Sarah's head dropped as the warm memories began to burn. "I miss them so much." Mary took her hand, and they sat in silence. Some of the days were going to be easier than others.

250

CHAPTER 26
Present
Sarah

Mary came over, started the coffee, and went in to help Sarah out of bed. She scanned the pictures along the shelves as she so often did in the past. When she looked back at Sarah, she was surprised to see a soft smile on her lips. Only a short time ago, Sarah would avoid looking directly at the pictures.

"Would you hand me the one of Kyle dressed in his overalls?" Mary knew better than to make a big deal of it and handed the picture to her. "He was incredibly handsome, wasn't he? He was going to be a good man, just like Andy."

"He was good. He had a good life. Yes, it was too short, but it was good."

Sarah was silent. Once Mary had her settled into her recliner with coffee in hand, she addressed the day's agenda.

"Your turn. What's on your list of to do's?" Sarah knew it was time for a big one.

"I guess it's time to get real with this plan, so here goes. I know I need to go to confession. It's what we Catholics do as you have reminded me. We go to church on Sundays and confession when we need to. It's just that...you're right. I have no clue what they're talking about anymore. I have felt dead to it for a very long time."

"What do you mean?"

"I used to go because my father made me, and then I wanted to go, and now it's just habit. It gave me peace and sometimes answers, but now..."

"Keep it coming." Sarah took a deep breath. It was strange talking so deeply, even with Mary.

"I keep going hoping to hear God. He doesn't talk to me anymore."

"Maybe it's just you're not in a place to hear Him. Maybe you need to look for Him somewhere else."

"And where do you suggest? Everything looks so black to me. Don't get me wrong. You're helping, but coal doesn't become a diamond overnight. It's just that after Kyle died, everywhere I looked, I saw sadness: it's all I've seemed to see since the accident. I watch the news. It's all about who murdered who, or how many people were killed in some tornado, or who was killed by a drunk driver. Where is He? He's not at church, and I sure as hell don't see Him anywhere else."

"Well, forgive me while I get deep for a minute, but how do you see the light without darkness? How would you know the difference if it was always light? Think about us as humans. We crave chaos, and in some ways, tragedy. We choose our movies and our books by the conflict in them. We're drawn to it. Maybe not so much if it's in our own lives. Sure, we all want something to gossip about, but we don't want a tragedy to find us. Well, it did find us, Sarah, and it stinks! Maybe though, in some unspeakable way, we needed it to find us. Heroes exist because conflict exists.

"You're sitting in your shell wondering where God is when maybe he's wondering when you're going to be a hero. When are you going to fight this off? Maybe he gave you Amanda and me to help you, and you're the one ignoring what He's putting right in front of you. You're so determined to be miserable that you refuse to see that He wants you to be happy. It wouldn't surprise me one bit if He's getting a bit impatient with you, too. Listen, Sarah; tragedy, loss, fear, depression, they all stink, but they're part of the package. We should have always known that and not wasted so much time getting pissed off about it."

"I think I was given a crappy package, Mary, and it's just...It's just so hard."

"Sarah, you stuck by me when things weren't good. My marriage was a sham until the day Dan died. You were always there for me. You were always strong, and it made me strong. I'm here now, but you must decide to be strong. I can't do it for you. Even if I have all the goodness in the world in me," Sarah raised an eyebrow at her, "if you don't choose to see it, then it didn't do you any good. Now did it?"

"I know you're right. It's just been so long I don't know how."

"Well, for one thing, we are going to declare everyday story day, and you're going to tell me something good. No crying allowed. Remember something good, and don't try to tie anything negative into it. Just live in a positive memory for a moment and be thankful for it."

Sarah sat silently for a moment before responding. "Have I ever told you about the day I met Andy?"

"About a hundred times, but who's counting?" Mary smiled at her friend. "Tell me a hundred more if you need to." The spring breeze pushed through the screen lifting the debris of the past with it. The afternoon went by with comfortable silences and more happy memories than either of them had recalled in a very long time.

FATHER ARGY AND SARAH

The next day, they walked into the church. It had a coolness to it like the fresh side of a pillow on a hot summer day. Father Argy was on the alter straightening items as if it were his home, which in many ways it was. He saw Mary struggle to hold the door and push the wheelchair through at the same time, and with a small smirk, ignored the words she uttered. Mary was the wayward student he couldn't help but adore. He reached them in time to catch the closing door and let it shut gently.

Brushing her slightly sweaty hair to the side, Mary spoke with heavy breath, "Sarah would like some help making her arrangements."

Father Argy had waited for a quiet moment with Sarah for so long and secretly thanked God for the opportunity.

"I'll tell you what Mary, why don't you run an errand, and I'll work out some things with Sarah. We'll fill you in when you get back. What do you say to about an hour?"

"She's all yours." She patted Sarah on the shoulder and assured her she would be back in that time. Then she turned on her heel, and for the moment, left the problems to someone better suited.

"How are you doing, Sarah?"

"I'm here to make funeral arrangements. Not that great."

Sarah and Mary had become a bit of a mystery to him throughout the years. He was a young priest in his thirties when he heard about Sarah's rape. He was the priest that prayed at her son's funeral with them, and since then, he watched Sarah, a shadow of herself, attend church every Sunday. First, with her husband, and then with Mary, a woman that avoided him whenever possible. He was drawn to them for reasons he could not understand.

"What would you like me to know?" Father Argy asked, inviting all possible answers.

"I want to be buried with my son and husband."

"Anything else?"

"I don't want an open casket. I don't want anyone looking at me when I'm dead."

"I understand."

He waited. He knew that these details were not his general business, but he sensed there was another need, so he listened. Several minutes passed, and he saw the jaw of this hardened woman begin to shake.

"I should probably go to confession."

"I can hear your confessions now if you like. Would you like to go to the confessional?" Sarah nodded.

Due to the wheelchair, Father Agry pushed her into a larger confessional where they sat face-to-face. Her heart beat upon her chest, and she wanted to cry out her desire to be hidden, even though she knew it was time to be seen.

She began with making the sign of the cross and saying, "Forgive me, Father, for I have sinned. It has been," Sarah paused and looked up at the priest, and he encouraged her with a nod, "a long time since my last confession." The silence lasted long enough for the priest to cross and uncross his legs several times.

"Sarah, what you say here is between you and God. It will not leave this room. I believe, for you to be at peace with yourself, you need to let God lift these sins from you." Sarah began to cry. Her shoulders lifted and fell, and a silent sob escaped her.

"I killed a man a very long time ago."

And with that, Sarah let the story leave her. She was surprised that once she started the story, from the rape to the accident, the words flowed from her.

She cried for several moments before the priest said, "Do you know why we do penance? It's not just to make it right with God. It's to make it right with ourselves. We cannot go to Heaven with the same guilt and hatred we felt here on earth. We need to prepare our spirits for the gifts God has in store for us. Sarah, for your penance, you need to make it right with the people that were hurt by your actions. Do this for yourself, Sarah, so that you can forgive yourself."

Father Argy said a few more routine prayers and then absolved her of her sins. Sarah sat for a moment, trying to let it settle in, knowing it was time to face her past. That night she called Amanda.

CHAPTER 27

Present
Sarah

Sarah smiled to herself, thinking of the conversation she had with her daughter the night before. She had barely gotten the words out of her mouth, asking her daughter to visit, when she swore that she heard the sound of a suitcase opening. For the first time in many years, Sarah was excited to get out of bed.

"Good morning," a youthful excitement sprang through Sarah as Mary entered her bedroom.

"What do you say we get you looking pretty for your daughter?" Sarah smiled and cried at the same time. "Tell me when you're finished crying, and I'll slap some make-up on that old face."

"I'm not sure I'm ever going to stop." She dried her eyes with a tissue as new tears rushed down her face.

"Maybe we should skip the make-up for now. Do you still own a curling iron?"

"I don't even know. Look under my sink." Mary found a curling iron that must have been thirty-years-old. She tentatively plugged it in and waited for sparks.

"I think it works. Let me know if you smell smoke." Soft, happy giggles flowed between them. They were again, two girls preparing for prom, nothing but excitement and promise awaited them.

"What time will she be here?"

"She said by lunch. Oh my! Do you think she likes Meals on Wheels lunches?"

"Oh, honey! I'll get you pretty and go out for sandwiches. We would like her to come back." Mary wheeled Sarah up to the mirror and started curling her sparse but now dark hair.

"Thank you, Mary." They smiled at each other in the mirror until the smell of burnt hair distracted them.

Sarah watched the clock tick until she heard the gravel in the driveway, the footfalls on the steps, the slight unnecessary knock, and the creak of the old screen door. She watched as a woman entered her home more beautiful than anything that she had ever dreamed of seeing. She clung to the image of her as it blurred behind tears until she felt Amanda embrace her. Suddenly, they were one mass, sturdy enough to withstand the breaking dam.

How had she let this happen? How had she shut her daughter out and wasted so many years? She stopped herself from allowing in the self-hatred and all the thoughts that went with it. She had spent too much time in that hell. She took her daughter's face in her hands and made herself look in her eyes.

259

"I'm sorry, Amanda. I'm so very sorry."

"It's okay. I'm just so glad you called me." After a moment more of holding each other, Amanda asked, "Does this mean that you are...that you...?"

"Let's pretend for the weekend that it doesn't. Let's just do the things we should have been doing."

Amanda answered through her tears, "Okay."

Mary entered, holding a bag from the local deli. "Am I interrupting?"

Amanda was quick to get up and embrace the woman who had secretly kept her involved in her mother's life. She was why her mother was not a stranger. She had waited for this moment as patiently as Mary had.

The weekend was spent with card games and movies, looking at photo albums and telling memories. Many times, Mary and Amanda would look over to find Sarah fast asleep, and they would exchange nervous glances until a subtle grunt or snore escaped, which left them with a smile.

Each week Amanda went home to her career, and each Friday, she returned, but within weeks she could see her mother spiraling downward. The time she spent awake became less frequent, and Amanda knew her time was precious. Sarah knew that it was time for the truth.

For weeks, seeing Amanda's smile whenever she entered the room was plagued by Sarah's need to repent. She was torn by what it would do to her daughter. If she told Amanda, she would add more pain to a life that had seen its share. The loss of a brother, the death of a father, and a mother that disappeared into the darkness should be enough for any person. Amanda would know that her mother was raped by her best friend's husband, that she sought revenge by taking his life, and in doing so, was responsible for her son's death.

Was knowledge always a good thing? Sarah ultimately decided that it was not a decision for her to make. She would let Amanda choose to remain in her world or step into the darker world that had destroyed her mother for decades.

Sarah sat down with a pen and paper and began to write. The letter would be sealed and given to her lawyer. The choice to read it or not would be Amanda's.

Amanda,

If you are reading this letter, I ask first for your forgiveness and understanding. It might be a request that is too much to dream of you honoring, but I will ask regardless.

Life is a strange combination of fate and choices, of forks in the road, with no clear direction, of blurred rationale and enlightenment.

My confession comes from bad decisions that first Mary's husband, Dan, made, and then I made myself. Dan was a man that was controlling and afflicted with alcoholism and hatred. These two things brought him to our house, where he chose to rape me. I lost myself after that. My hatred for him made it acceptable for me, in my mind, to tamper with his car.

I wasn't sure what would happen. I told myself if it led to Dan's death, then he well-deserved it. If it just led to a scare, then I would make other decisions. I wanted him dead. I could not stand the thought of seeing him every day around the people I loved. I couldn't stand to hear one more rumor about what he did behind Mary's back or watch one of our neighbors become his next victim. He was an evil man, but I had no right. God should have been the final judge as to when his days should end.

You might have realized by now that I also caused Kyle's death. I had no idea Kyle would be in that car. Dan had never offered him a ride before, which is a fact that made me so bitter for years. I felt God had punished me by taking away my son. I hated myself as you may hate me right now.

I hope that you not only forgive me for destroying our family with my hatred but for pushing you away. I hated myself so much that looking at you hurt. I didn't even realize it at times; I just couldn't be near you. What I have lost, the years I let slip by, I missed your life because I hated myself so much.

The third thing I need you to forgive me for is for forgiving myself. If you are reading this letter and are despising me right now, it may sicken you to know that I have finally forgiven myself. I hope, though, that someday this brings you peace as you approach an age where forgiveness is so important. At this point, to me, it is everything.

I don't believe that I need to say goodbye anymore because I feel for the first time in a long time that we will go on, and it will be good. I have always and will always love you.

Mom

Sarah sealed the envelope and put it with the rest of the papers for her lawyer. She felt she had made the right choice.

Amanda came in the door the next Friday. Sarah smiled at how quickly the sound had become natural again. It was as if she had not missed hundreds of doors opening through the years; it was as if she had always welcomed her in. Children were born to love their parents, even if they were undeserving. She was thankful for that.

"I'm here, and I brought treats." Amanda pulled out two Danishes and coffee.

"Mmm...they look delicious." It was an innocent lie.

Amanda pulled a kitchen chair up to her rolling table and had a seat next to her. Her skin glowed, and excitement rolled off her as if Sarah was a gift. Sarah watched her bite into the warm Danish, closing her eyes to allow the full flavor to melt in her mouth.

"Amanda, I'm so glad that you were willing to accept me back. You mean everything to me."

Tears welled in Amanda's eyes, and a rush of pain hit Sarah. She never believed she would allow those words to surprise her child. She should have always known.

"Mom, I wouldn't be anywhere else." The quiet that followed was beautiful and natural, although Sarah knew it was time for her to mention the letter.

"I have to tell you something," said Sarah.

"Anything, Mom. Tell me anything."

"I have been doing a lot of thinking about my life and the choices that I've made. I want you to know that my depression had nothing to do with you. I have said it before, but I want you to completely understand that you had nothing to do with it."

"I believe you, Mom, but you know you can tell me whatever it is that made you so depressed. I always believed it was Kyle's accident and," her eyes automatically dropped away as she continued, "the rape, but apparently, it was more than that. I'll listen. I'll listen to everything."

"I want you first to know that my secrets have been kept secret for reasons partly for me and partly for the people I love." Sarah stopped as she often did to catch her breath. "I've struggled with what to do and how it would affect you. I've decided to write you a letter that will be kept by my lawyer. Whenever you choose to know, the information is there for you."

Amanda stared at her for a moment. "Do you think I should read it?"

"Honestly, no, I don't. Not for myself, although there may be a bit of me that fears how it will change what you think of me, but because no good will come of it. It'll hurt you and your image of me and what you need my image to be like as your mother. I wrote it because it's your right to know. It's not your obligation."

"Okay. Do I have to decide by any given time?"

"The letter will be there until you pass. Then it will be destroyed." Amanda nodded her head. The remnants of her Danish forgotten.

"Amanda, there are many important truths, but the only truth that I see important to your life is that you are loved and always were. The other truths are like finding out what lurked under the water that rocked your boat. Besides curiosity, is there any reason you need to know what it was if you will never travel down that path again? It is up to you, and I understand whatever decision you make."

"Well, I guess we will leave it at that for now. Would you like to see what's on television?

As if on call Drew Carey, was there again, standing at the wheel with a contestant. She'd spun an eighty and was trying to decide to risk going on. Sarah wondered if she saw the hint in his eyes, telling her to stay right where she was.

Sarah knew that it was time to tell Mary the terrible truths that had destroyed her for so long. What she didn't realize was how limited her time had become.

FINAL CHAPTER
Mary

Hospice was coming in and out of the house throughout the day doing whatever Amanda and Mary could not do for Sarah and adding relief when needed. Amid it all, Mary received a phone call from Eva's husband, announcing that she was in labor.

Mary threw together some things and ran to her car. She stopped to look at Sarah's home. There was a storm cloud moving in, but Amanda was home. There was still so much to be said. The hardest things took the longest, and she waited patiently for Sarah to be ready. She drove down the gravel driveway hoping there was time.

SARAH

Sarah had Amanda push her chair outside when she saw the approaching storm. They sat side by side, holding hands.

"This porch has seen many things, hasn't it?"

"Yes, it has. I'm surprised you're out here during a storm. Dad would be impressed."

Sarah smiled to herself. "I'm not afraid anymore."

They spent the evening watching the lightning as if it were a show put on just for them.

In her dream, she was floating on her back, looking up at the stars. There was only peace around her. The water licked at her sides and deafened her ears, so she heard nothing and everything at the same time. She was happy. There was no fear of what was beneath her or above her; she floated effortlessly in her place. Even when she began to sink, there was no fear, only the feeling that she couldn't breathe. She felt herself coughing and thought it was an oddly human reaction, but still could not control it. Then the dream disappeared.

She would learn later that Amanda heard her mother in the night and came to her bedside. When she couldn't awaken her, she called the ambulance. When Sarah next opened her eyes, she found Amanda by her bedside at the hospital, just as it should have been. Sarah struggled to speak, but Amanda quieted her and explained what happened. Sarah began to panic. She needed to talk to Mary.

"Mary? Did you call Mary?"

"Yes, Mom. She's on her way."

Sarah stared at the machines, watching the evidence of life across the monitor. She desperately offered a prayer that Mary would make it in time to hear her final confession. The monitor beeped on as

Sarah struggled to keep her breaths slow and steady. Her time was almost at hand.

Amanda sensed her desperation. She rubbed her mother's forearm and told her she would go out and watch for her. The seconds were ticking away too quickly, and she felt herself fading.

From out in the hallway, Sarah heard the familiar, but speedier, clicking of heels approaching. Mary raced around the corner in an uncharacteristic fluster. Dropping her purse in a chair, she was at Sarah's bedside in a moment. Talking was a struggle, but Sarah knew she had to find the words.

"Mary," she continued through her raspy breathing, "I have to tell you something."

"Don't try to talk."

"No, I have to tell you, or I can't go in peace."

"Sarah, you damned fool. Do you think I would have stuck by your depressing butt if I didn't already know?" Mary's voice was cracking, and she tried hard to hold it together. Sarah stared at her in disbelief. "I found the bag of stolen artifacts in a closet. Dan must have hidden them there. After the funeral, I threw it in the pond. I saw you that night in my driveway. I didn't know what you were doing for sure, but I've pieced it together pretty well."

"Why didn't you tell me? All these years you knew and didn't tell me."

"Maybe for the same reason you didn't tell me. Some things are too hard. I was ready to listen if you needed to talk. I waited. The days turned into months, then years. I felt such shame for bringing this into our lives. I didn't want to lose you to prison, but I lost you anyway. I felt by leaving it alone, it would all go away. Instead, you just went away from me, from Amanda, from the world for so long. I tried to bring you back. I tried to be patient. It took so long."

Both women let the tears start to slide down their cheeks.

Sarah stared at her friend in a new light. "Wouldn't you know it. Even sin looks better on you."

"Do you see? I never needed to forgive you. I needed you to forgive me. I would have done anything for that. I think about how different our lives would have been if I made different choices. I put you in the spot you were in, so I'm as guilty as you. What I could never figure out is why, why did he have to go after you?"

"I found it. First. I tried. To get him to leave."

"Why would you do that? Why would you confront a monster?"

"To protect. You. And the girls."

"Well, aren't we a couple of fools?" The sound of Sarah's labored breathing filled the air. Mary had walked with her through purgatory to find her

270

salvation. Sarah's life began to make sense, and her shallow breaths eased.

"Maybe life didn't turn out that bad after all. Just different than we expected," said Mary.

"Quite different." The two women smiled at each other, bonded by a deep wisdom.

"Thank you for never giving up." With a last effort, Sarah said, "I'll see you on the other side."

"I believe you will, my friend."

Mary held tighter to Sarah's hand. This friend of hers took her hand and walked her as close to the door as she was allowed. Sarah wasn't afraid because she knew that, as in life, she was being handed over and not let go of. The next hand to take hers would be wearing a baseball mitt. Sarah would join in their game as if she had just walked off her back porch and into her yard, a yard full of love greater than she had ever experienced because secrets no longer mattered.

She took with her not a chain and concrete blocks, but an understanding that life is a gift just as much as a box wrapped in silver adorned with golden ribbons. It doesn't matter that inside the box is despair and darkness, pain, and tragedy because mixed in with all of it are love and laughter and the greatest gift of all, forgiveness. Forgiveness for trying your best and still falling short. She gave thanks for these lessons taught in a hard school, and, for the first time in a very long time, she stood unwounded and unburdened. She squeezed Mary's hand and slipped away.

EPILOGUE

Amanda stood in the living room that saw her mother through so many years. Memories overwhelmed her, the warm ones, the bitter ones, the confused and neglected ones. So many years, Amanda had wondered as she cried privately. Where did my mother go? What had she done to be shunned by her for so long?

She stared down at the envelope in her hand. She received it with the deed to the house, each item containing a piece of the woman she loved. In one hand, there was the house with the shared memories, of cooking and playing house, of styling hair and picking out clothes, of laughing and crying and holding and sharing and then emptiness.

The emptiness sat in the envelope in the other hand, the missing piece of the puzzle. On the front was printed only her name. Not for Amanda, or to Amanda, just Amanda. Her mother had told her it was her right, but not her obligation to read what Sarah had written. She looked around the house that, even though it was barren, now showed the memories of a lifetime. The only real memories that Amanda cared to have. When she tore the envelope in pieces, she felt the power of the demons subside, leaving only the warmth of her childhood home behind. She closed the door behind her, taking with her all that was important.

The End

Acknowledgements

I would like to thank my father-in-law, George Tripp, and my sister, Kim Stone, for being there for me as the story took form. I also want to thank my brave friends that were willing to give me their honest opinions: Lisa Lynch, Gretchen Hurley, Donna Nuckols, Cathy Klein, Shawn Vernon, Lisa Cascanette, and Debbie Ramer. Also, thanks to my parents, John and Gail Sheehan, for helping me look at the world with a greater understanding and appreciation of everything. I love you both.

Made in the USA
Monee, IL
13 February 2020